The Hyde Hotel

The Hyde Hotel

Proprietors: James Everington & Dan Howarth

BLACK
SHUCK
BOOKS

Black Shuck Books
www.blackshuckbooks.co.uk

First published in the UK in 2016 by
Black Shuck Books,
Kent, UK

Please sign the Guestbook

Checking In

You can't remember where you heard about the Hyde Hotel – you mentioned to someone you were staying in this city and they recommended it to you, perhaps. Not someone you know well, a friend of a friend. You have scribbled down some details of the booking you must have made over the phone – unusual for you, someone who does everything online nowadays. You prefer to avoid human contact, human voices; you prefer to travel alone. But when you exit the train station the directions you have written down bear no resemblance to the layout of the streets around you. Your phone stubbornly refuses to understand the postcode when you type it in.

"The Hyde?" people say when you ask for directions. "Oh yeah, *that* place." For some reason they all feel compelled to tell you their opinion of it whilst they are trying to remember how to get there: you are variously told that it is old and needs some serious renovation and that it is new and ghastly; that it is tall and overbearing and that it is squat and hidden; that it is down by the canal, that it is in the old town, that it is near this square or that church...

"It's just down King's Walk and on your left..."

"It's back up the hill and left onto Caxton Road and then..."

"The Hyde? You must have just walked right past it..."

It's almost as if they are making it up; you suppose people in this city (which you have never been to before) just don't want to admit they can't help you. And after all, who really knows about the hotels in their home town?

Nevertheless, as you are blown in different directions trying to find it, as you cross and re-cross your path following people's conflicting and opposing directions, you start to build up an image in your head of the Hyde, a composite of all the things people are telling you, plus your own imaginations and fancies too. It's nondescript, a cheap hotel for those travelling on their own, without the luxury of an expenses account.

When you eventually find it, by luck rather than anything else, it is almost exactly as you pictured it. It is on the street that the last person you asked, an older man with the same holdall as you, told you it was.

Tired and hot after the ridiculous amount of time it took you to find it, you wearily head towards the reception desk. It is dark in the Hyde after the sunlight outside, and in the shadows it takes you a few seconds to realise the desk is unmanned. There is an old-fashioned bell on the desk; when you ring it, the sound is like something you heard once on an old TV show or film.

It is a long time before anyone comes.

The walk to your room is long and you are sure the receptionist, whoever he or she was, has told you a needlessly confusing route. You are too tired to care or to wonder at the odd pattern in the carpet or the note shoved under the door of one of the rooms as you pass. At why your nose itches as if full of dust, or why an open window you pass smells of the sea despite the Hyde being as far inland as you can get. You just want to get to your room.

When you eventually do, it holds no surprises. A typical cheap hotel room, magnolia walls and hastily assembled furniture. Everything in it, from the bed to the curtains to the worn towels, seemingly comes from the same set of four or five neutral colours. A kettle and sachets of instant drinks from which all but the decaf coffee is missing. No phone signal. A dirty window – when you look out of it the streets you can see bear no resemblance to the route you remember taking here, and it has darkened so quickly the weather seems that of a different place entirely. You try and open the window for some air, but as you expected it is stuck. You've stayed in plenty of similar rooms before, alone, and this instant feels like a composite of all those times before – your life measured out in pay-to-view porn and plastic teaspoons. Nevertheless, there is one thing odd about this room, despite how closely it tallies with what you were imagining.

There are no mirrors anywhere, not in the room itself or the bathroom.

But the thought of going back to reception to change rooms is wearying in itself, and besides you are only here for one night. The people you are seeing tomorrow will scarcely care about your appearance.

Suddenly exhausted, and sweating as if with start of a fever, you sit on the bed and realise you are almost falling asleep. There are faint, odd noises coming through the thin walls from the adjoining room, but you feel too tired to care. Annoyed with yourself, and in an effort to focus your mind on something to keep yourself awake, you stand and reach for the hotel information pack on the small desk.

What *are* they doing next door? you think as you open the leaflet.

The Hyde Hotel Welcomes YOU, it says.

James Everington

The View from the Basement

The Hyde Hotel looked like the sort of place a travelling salesman might use, and Leslie Baines should know, for a travelling salesman is what he was. Now though, he was on holiday, and he set his bag down next to his feet and ran his grey eyes over the grey exterior. It was the first time he'd been on holiday to a city, and the first time without his wife.

The sign saying 'Hyde Hotel' gave a dispirited flash, as if electricity had sparked through it before giving up the ghost. Leslie took it as an invitation. He picked up his bag and went inside. The reception desk looked much the same as those in all the other hotels he'd ever stayed in. Behind it was a bored looking lad, probably not yet out of his teens. His head was shaved at the back and long on top and a silver stud shone in his eyebrow. Leslie approached. The lad wore a name badge, but his name wasn't on it. Instead it said *A.N. Assistant Manager*. He imagined, if he came back in a week, someone else would be sitting there, wearing that same badge and that same expression.

It seemed to pain the boy to lift his head from the magazine he was reading, which appeared to be about fast cars. He didn't say anything, and his expression didn't change. Leslie found himself thinking he looked like the kind of kid who'd have lusted from afar at all the hot girls in school, but he'd never once have dared to speak to them. If he had, they wouldn't have known his name. He was the kind of kid Leslie could recognise all too well.

Leslie realised that no one had spoken for a little too long. He said, "This *is* the Hyde Hotel?"

"Oh, yes *sir*. You've most definitely come to the right place."

Leslie frowned. Now he thought this was probably the kind of kid who'd have fantasised, all through his senior year, about murdering his classmates. He might even have written stories about it; stories that weren't very good.

The boy held something out. It was a key-card, but with a hole in the corner attached to a loop of twine as if it was a regular key, a mingling of past and present. Attached to the loop was a rough wooden block that looked as if it could conceivably have been used to brain somebody.

Leslie took it. He didn't say thank you. He just shuffled away towards a sign that said *LIFT*.

~

There was a picture in the lift. It looked like one of those motivational things, the sort that should have writing underneath meant to cheer people up or spur them on, but which instead left them feeling mildly depressed. 'Bless all our tomorrows' or 'Love is forever' or some such crap. This one was of sunset over water, except, when Leslie looked again, it wasn't quite like that. The sky was red and bloody, but he couldn't see the sun. The water was purple and dark. *Sunless*, he thought. That's what it was: *sunless*, like in that Coleridge poem.

Then he saw there was writing on the poster after all, *LESURE CLUB*, like that, with one letter missing. *There's no I in Club*, he thought, smothering a giggle.

"Floor?"

Leslie let out a noise that was a little like a yelp. He hadn't realised there was someone in the lift with him until they'd spoken. He turned. The man wore a dark suit; he looked a little like a travelling salesman. But of course, Leslie must have seen him when he first got in. He'd simply assumed the figure was his own reflection, but there was no mirror in the lift, and anyway, Leslie wasn't wearing his suit; he was on holiday.

He consulted the numbers on his wooden block. "Second," he said, and the man pressed the button and they began to clank and whirr their way upward.

~

The room wasn't all that a hotel room could be. Leslie remembered the last holiday his wife, Carol, had arranged. She knew how to organise a holiday, did Carol. She'd have telephoned in advance and got them a better view than they'd paid for. There'd have been a pool, maybe even a spa. She'd have got extras. There would have been a banana sitting in the cracked fruit-bowl on the coffee-stained table; maybe even an orange. Leslie shrugged. He'd never troubled about such things when he was alone, but then, those trips were planned by the office. This one was his.

He tried to open the window for some air, but an old paint job had sealed it shut. He let the yellowing net curtain fall back across the view of the rear yard and its collection of metal bins. The cracked concrete on which they stood was strewn with cigarette butts, though no one was smoking there now. He went into the tiny bathroom. There was a bar of soap by the sink, unboxed and worn around the edges, its centre fractured with deep grey cracks. There were no extras, unless he counted the nailbrush sitting on the ledge by the bath, its remaining bristles resembling the curled legs of dead flies. He found himself placing his toiletries bag on the floor under the sink, leaving the shelf free for *her*; then he stood and put it on the shelf instead.

Carol, he thought, would have liked the kind of poster he'd seen in the lift. Or rather, she would have liked *him* to like it. For him to conform, to fit in; to succeed.

He shook his head as if to clear it of the echo of her nagging voice, and went to take a look around the city he'd pitched up in. He was, he reminded himself, on holiday.

~

Leslie bought a map. He wandered around the things that tourists were supposed to be interested in. He stood and looked at the pigeons breeding on the north face of the cathedral. He saw the statue of the city's founding father, looking fat and pompous in the square. He ate a dry scone in the museum cafe, staring out of the window at a teacher trying to herd her recalcitrant wards onto a coach.

Then he went back to the hotel.

Just as he entered reception, thinking *She would have known how to get the best room*, he was hailed by a voice. "Mr Baines."

His insides froze. He felt as if he'd done something wrong and now he was caught and everything was going to end. He couldn't turn around. Then the same teenager he'd seen before poked his metal stud into his face.

"Been trying to tell you. Double booked. Had to move you."

Leslie started to breathe again. How odd, that he should react in such a way. He reminded himself that he was the guest, that he should be spoken to in a fashion befitting–

The lad pushed something into his hand. It was a key, looking much like the first, except this time the numbers were different. *She would have known how to get the best room*, he thought, and he started to smile.

In the lift, when he consulted the numbers again, his smile faded. He thought he'd have been moved upward, onto the dizzy heights of the third floor perhaps, maybe even higher, but he had not. The first number on the key was a minus. He scanned the row of buttons until he found the one with a B for Basement, and he pressed it, and he began to descend.

The lift opened onto a long corridor that had once, long ago, been painted white. Fluorescent lights flickered and buzzed. Leslie was unsurprised to see that his room lay in the direction of the hotel's rear yard. The back of the hotel must be lower than the side that faced the street, because he could see daylight through the door at the end of the passage; he could just see the bins, distorted through its glass panes.

He started to walk down the corridor. There was a ringing sound in his ears. No: a squeaking, regular and rhythmic, that made him think of the tricycle in *The Shining*. When he got into his room, which was much like the first but smaller and hotter and without any windows, he found his things had been moved for him. His bag was positioned on his side of the bed. His toiletries bag was placed next to the sink, on the floor. There was nothing on the shelf at all.

~

Leslie had married his wife because she was a prize he coveted. Once he had her, he found she bored him after all. Later, it was more than that.

His wife thought he was selfish. "Leslie," she'd say, "you're selfish." That was how he knew. She'd say he should try harder at work so he could buy her things. She said he wasn't any good at anything. She said he should notice her, which was odd, because he couldn't avoid noticing her. He had wished he could, many times.

He closed his eyes. He saw earth beneath his fingernails; he wasn't sure why. He thought of that nailbrush, its dead-fly bristles, and he grimaced.

He shook himself. He was on holiday. He would go down for dinner. He changed his shirt, straightening his hair in the mirror – his skin looked grey in that mirror, his eyes pouchy – and he thought about ordering something really fattening, *with too many numbers*, as she would have put it, followed by something else really fattening.

He smiled as the lift ascended. He tried a whistle. It mingled with the discordant groans of the lift cables, and he stopped. He looked at the buttons and noticed that they had changed. LESURE CLUB, one of them said now, though that hadn't been there before, had it? Or maybe the button had, and only the sign was new.

He peered at it. It didn't look new. The writing was faded and pink against a dull purple background. Then the door opened, and he forgot about it and headed towards the dining room.

There weren't many tables left. One in the corner was free, next to someone who looked like a travelling salesman. Another was adjacent to an old woman seated by the far wall, focused on her knitting. He went over to the table next to hers. A girl came and took his order and he waited. He couldn't hear any conversation, only the *clack-clack, clack-clack* of knitting needles. Leslie made sure not to catch anyone's eye. He couldn't be bothered with polite chit-chat; it was too much like work. Instead he examined the ceiling, and then the mismatched chairs, and then the floor.

It was only when the clacking stopped that he glanced at the woman seated next to him. She had turned in her seat, was watching him. Her stare was intense, her face more lined than any face should be, her grey hair diaphanous around it. She leaned towards him and opened her mouth. There was a smell. He tried not to recoil.

"You're selfish, Leslie," she said, and Leslie rocked back in his own seat, his mouth falling open.

"What?" he said. "What did you say?" But the woman had gone back to her knitting. She didn't even look at him, just kept moving her hands, the needles flying, *clack-clack, clackety-clack*, the knitting spilling from her table and pooling at her feet, the wool as grey and fine as cobwebs.

A plate banged onto the table in front of him and Leslie jumped. He looked down. He opened his mouth to tell the waitress *No, that's not my order*, but she had already gone. He sighed. He didn't have his curry; he didn't have any chips. Instead there was a small piece of grilled fish on a few limp lettuce leaves and thin slices of watery-looking potato. He realised, dismally, that it was Carol's favourite.

He picked up a fork and poked at the fish. The outside was coated with black crumbs; he wasn't sure if they were supposed to be there or if they were something the fish had picked up from the pan. Inside, the flesh looked wet, almost raw. *Still wriggling*, he thought, and that reminded him of something and he pushed the idea away before it could take form. His head was beginning to ache. He no longer felt hungry.

He put a piece of potato in his mouth anyway and began to chew. Almost at once he spat it out onto the plate. It was green inside, and hard, and it had a funny taste; a bad taste. He looked up. The waitress was watching him, contempt written across her features.

"It's rotten," he said.

She leaned in and looked at it. "Looks fine to me," she

said, though it clearly wasn't fine, it was half-chewed food spat onto the plate. "Nothing wrong with it." And then: "She'd have made sure it was perfect."

"*What* did you say?"

"Said there's nothing wrong with it. Want it or not?"

Leslie looked at the plate. Something about it made him shudder. He decided that 'not' was definitely the better option. He glanced at the table next to his as he stood to leave, but at some point during his dinner, the old woman had left.

Descending to his room in the lift, he noticed that the LESURE CLUB button had gone. Maybe it kept falling off; maybe, later, the bored teenager from reception would come along and stick it back on again.

~

Leslie had forgotten to bring toothpaste. He ran his tongue over his teeth. Something was sticking to them, probably that awful stuff he'd put into his mouth earlier. He should go and complain. He should demand they provide toothpaste, free and with their bloody compliments, and they shouldn't expect him to pay for dinner.

He pushed himself up, feeling sick. He couldn't purge the taste of dead things from his mouth. When he got to the lift, he found the doors were blocked; a maid was trying to manoeuvre a laundry cage into it. He squeezed inside after her. The laundry gave off a stink that belied the hotel's claim of *Fresh sheets every day*. It mingled with the taste in his mouth. He felt suddenly faint and he sagged, leaning against the wall, squeezing his eyes closed. When he opened them again, the maid's face was up close to his.

"You're no good, Leslie," she said. "You don't try. You go to work but you don't get anywhere. You don't like the posters, Leslie."

He swallowed hard, pushing down the sour taste. The words went on, and went on some more. He felt they were sticking to him, surrounding him, like cobwebby wool, like a cloud of floating hair. He couldn't breathe. He was being smothered. No: he was drowning, drowning in words, drowning in her disgust, her contempt, her *hate*.

Love is forever, he thought, and suddenly he wanted to laugh, and that was better. He straightened. The maid wasn't even looking at him. She was looking into the air, somewhere above the doors. She was chewing gum. It was as if he wasn't there at all.

He took a deep breath. Carol had said once, on a holiday that was a little but not quite like this, that she would hate to be drowned. *It must be awful*, she'd said, *just awful*, and it occurred to Leslie that if he could remind her of that now, if she could think at all, it would make her happy.

He shook his head. What on earth was wrong with him? Of course his wife could think. It wasn't as if—

He felt sick again. The lift doors slid open and he staggered out, into a corridor. He was back in the basement. The lights flickered and buzzed. Through the glass panels in the doors at the end, he could see a faint purple glow.

He forced himself to walk, as steadily as he could, back to his room. Food poisoning; perhaps that was it.

She'd never have allowed that, he thought, as he fell in through the door and pushed it closed behind him.

~

Leslie couldn't remember going upstairs. He remembered crossing reception, weaving in and out of all the people who suddenly seemed to be thronging the hotel. Perhaps there was a convention, he thought; perhaps it was for travelling salesmen.

"You should try harder," a woman with big dangly earrings said before he ducked out of her way, into the course of a mother with a young boy.

The mother said, "If only you weren't so selfish."

A cleaner said, "Just bloody eat it, I made it for you."

An old man said, "You don't notice me any more."

Leslie stumbled into the dining room, which was now the breakfast room, and he spooned cornflakes into his mouth. When he'd done, the man who took his dish away said, "Your name's not Baines. You only told us that."

Leslie stared after him. He felt cold, all over. He felt frozen, like the ground: the hard, unforgiving ground. He looked down at his hands. For a moment he saw dark earth, embedded under his nails; then it was gone.

"She's not dead," said the old woman with the knitting. She gave a soft laugh, each spurt of it like a last breath, *uh-uh-uh*. "Of course she's not dead!"

"I'm on holiday," said Leslie, his voice too loud. "Holiday!"

His vision cleared. A face was looking at him, full of wariness and not a little contempt. It was a man in a suit. He looked a bit like someone who would work in sales.

"My name's Baines," Leslie said. "If they ask. Baines!"

The man backed away. He couldn't seem to move fast enough.

Leslie put his hand to his head. He pushed himself up to leave the table and went in search of the lift. When he reached it, the button that said LESURE CLUB was back. The doors closed. The lift clanked and began to descend.

~

As soon as Leslie stepped into the basement corridor, he felt better. The lights still flickered but the air was cooler and his headache dissipated at once. He didn't feel like going back into his room though, that small box, and shutting himself inside. Somehow he couldn't bear the thought of it. Instead he went past his door and kept going, the lights buzzing louder than ever, and he went to the door at the end of the corridor, the white door. Its windows were of textured glass backed by wire mesh. He put out his hand to the push bar, expecting an alarm to shriek when he pressed on it, but there was no sound; none at all. Even the buzzing of the lights was suddenly cut off, as if he'd already stepped outside and closed it behind him.

She'd have had a pool, he thought, and he wanted to laugh because a pool was there after all. He must have pressed the wrong button; he was at the LESURE CLUB, except wasn't this where the bins were supposed to be? He must have got off at the wrong floor, got turned around somehow.

But when he looked out at the water, he saw it wasn't a pool after all. He didn't know how it was possible, but he couldn't even see its opposite edge. The water was dull and purple-grey and it shifted in an uneasy rhythm, and Leslie instinctively knew that there were dead things in it, if indeed anything could ever have lived in such a drear, lifeless place. It was a sea outside the back door of the Hyde Hotel; a sea where no sea should be.

He turned and looked back into the corridor. It was a perfectly ordinary corridor, but now there were people standing in it. They were staring at him, peering over one another's shoulders to see him better. For a moment he thought his wife was among them; then he blinked and they were gone.

He turned back to the sea. He felt better when he was looking at the sea. It wasn't that it made him feel happy; more that he didn't feel anything at all. It filled his vision with its emptiness. Its surface was completely opaque. *Anything could be in there,* he thought. *It could be covering anything, and they'd never be found again. Never be dug up.*

Sunless.

He shook his head and smiled. He was on holiday, wasn't he? He was on holiday and this was a LESURE CLUB, and he should be taking advantage. Availing himself of the facilities. He slipped the jacket from his shoulders and let it fall. Then he didn't move. He stood there for a long time, and he heard a sound and looked behind him.

The man who looked like a travelling salesman was standing in the corridor. There was a policeman with him. As Leslie watched, the salesman pointed towards him, mouthing something he couldn't hear.

Leslie slammed the door. Instantly, the corridor went

dark. He couldn't see anything through the windows at all.

Then he turned and waded into the water.

At first, it was cold. Then it wasn't cold any longer. It was the exact same temperature as his skin, and it opened, and it accepted him. The pool was sloping at the bottom, a ramp not steps, and it felt like tiles under his feet but then he began to sink into it and he realised it was mud sucking at his toes, pulling at his shoes. He stepped on one heel and pulled the shoe off, then prised the other free with his muddy sock. He knew he wouldn't find his shoes again; it didn't matter. He kept moving, the water lapping up to his knees and then his thighs. Before long, he was up to his neck. *Not cold*, he thought, *not like words*, and he didn't feel anything at all and that was good. He kept on walking. He didn't trouble to look back at all the things he was leaving behind.

Alison Littlewood

Night Porters

"I believe I have a reservation," Wilson said.

The hotel receptionist trailed a pale yellow fingernail down a list of names and then looked up, her finger paused at the bottom of the page.

"Oh sorry, yes, would help, wouldn't it – Wilson."

She dragged her nail down to the bottom of the page again. Wilson couldn't help but watch, waiting for her to pause on a name. He was too hot and slightly dizzy, and the yellow of her nail varnish made him think of infection.

"Not seeing you, Mr…"

"Wilson."

"Wil-son," she said, as if she were tasting every syllable, rolling them around in her mouth before spitting them out. "Wil-son. No." She looked up and smiled. "You don't appear to exist, Mr Wilson."

"It often feels that way," he said, and she just sat there, her finger on the page as if she had to hold it in place or it would float away. Wilson blinked sweat out of his eyes and wondered if it was making his bald head embarrassingly shiny.

A door opened behind the receptionist, and a very tall man slid through the door as if he were on rails. "Good evening sir," he said, and smiled a smile that made

Wilson feel uneasy. "I'm the general manager. Welcome to the Hyde Hotel. Do we have a problem, Eleanor, I do so apologise if we do, would be most unusual, so do we, Eleanor, do we have a problem?" He bent abruptly over the receptionist's shoulder, making her lean out of the way. Wilson thought that it was to look at the list, but the man unexpectedly shot a hand out over the reception desk and Wilson shook it then wished he hadn't.

"Mr Wilson thinks he has a reservation," the receptionist said, still tilting to one side as if it were the most natural thing in the world. "But he's not on the list."

"I'm sorry," Wilson said, and surreptitiously wiped his hand on his coat. "My employer was supposed to book it. I do hope..."

"Not a problem, sir. Eleanor, give him two ten. Perfect room for you sir, gentleman like yourself, I would say it's one of our better rooms but I wouldn't like to do the others down. Two-ten, Eleanor." The general manager straightened up from the counter, and rested his hand on the receptionist's head for a moment in a strange gesture that was neither pat nor stroke, then nodded to Wilson and disappeared back behind the door.

"Two ten," the receptionist said, and slid Wilson an off-white tag that was three times bigger than the key to which it was attached. "Breakfast at seven. Stairs to your right. Or you could take the lift." Her tone of voice implied that he probably shouldn't, and she didn't elaborate on where it was anyway. "Enjoy your stay at the Hyde, Mr Wilson."

"Thank you, Eleanor," he said, and then he worried that he was being over-familiar and she would think less of him. He wouldn't enjoy the stay. But it was what he did. Wilson picked up his case, and took the stairs.

A heavy fire door on the second landing was labelled 201-249. Wilson pushed the door open and nearly hit a man who was standing in the corridor, staring along it.

"Sorry," Wilson said.

"My fault," the man said. "Standing right in front of the door." He cocked his head one way, then another, squinted. "But look, can you see it? Or is it just me?"

Wilson looked along the empty corridor. "I'm sorry," he said. "See…"

"This carpet," the man said. "The pattern. Does it spell out words? Can you see it?"

Wilson put his case down. The carpet was patterned with a dense weave of multi-coloured lines that swirled and wiggled the length of the corridor.

"I can see why you'd think so," Wilson said. "But I can't make anything out. It's just a pattern, repeating."

The man nodded. "Must just be me then. Tired eyes."

"What did you think it said?"

"Couldn't quite make it out, but you know when you're trying to remember someone's name, and it's right on the tip of your tongue? Or one of those magic eye pictures where you spend ten minutes squinting, and can't ever see the stupid bicycle? Bit like that. Ah, well." The man turned and pushed through the fire door to the stairs. Wilson looked at the carpet for a moment or two longer, then picked up his case and walked along the corridor to 210.

~

He unpacked once and rearranged his things three times, trying to make the best use of the various drawers and shelves. It didn't make it feel like home, but then Wilson travelled so much that home didn't feel like home either. He spent weeks in hotel rooms that could be in any hotel, in any city, and then he returned home to his flat with magnolia walls and pictures in neat wooden frames and the bed linen smartly arranged, just like it had been when he left. Once, he had thought about making his flat different, painting the walls in vivid colours, haunting galleries full of the kind of interesting people that he had once wanted to be until someone engaged him in conversation and recommended some stunning artwork. But like most things, he couldn't really be bothered with it further. Wilson found that the best way to get through life. Don't think about things too much, and definitely don't bother with them. That and gin.

He ate a sandwich that he'd bought on the train, and after he'd finished it realised that unless he went back into the bin for the packet he couldn't have said what had been in it. Although his first meeting with the client wasn't until mid-morning Wilson liked to be finished with his preparation the night before, so he sat reading and making notes until it was well after midnight. When he'd put the papers back in his briefcase, he sat on the end of the bed and turned the TV on. Flicked through channels. Turned the TV off. Sat and read the room information again. Gave in to the inevitable. There was no point trying to sleep because he knew the signs, and he knew what he would do to cure it. Wilson picked up his wallet and key and left his room to head downstairs.

The bar was on the opposite side of the lobby to the stairs, but as soon as Wilson reached the ground floor he could see that the bar was dark and empty. Fair enough, he thought. Middle of the week. Middle of winter. Nearly one in the morning. Then he heard a cough, and jumped. A small man sat behind the reception counter, in some kind of maroon uniform jacket. He had wavy grey hair, which would be unruly if he let it grow any further.

"Oh, you gave me a fright," Wilson said. "Sorry, was just hoping against hope that the bar would still be serving."

"Evening sir," the man said. "I'm the night porter."

"Evening. Wilson. 210. I'm staying here." Wilson often felt the need to explain himself, and then felt foolish when he did.

"Of course, sir. Were you wishing for a drink?"

"No, no." Wilson felt a familiar heat in his cheeks. Why had he said that? The night porter would either know that he was lying, or think that he was prowling round the hotel up to no good. "Well, actually, just a nightcap. Have trouble sleeping."

"That's quite all right sir," the night porter said. "I can get you a drink. You're a resident."

"Well, I wouldn't want to put you to any bother."

The man stood up. He wasn't much bigger standing up than sitting down. "I'm the night porter. It's what I'm here for, sir. It's my purpose, if you like."

"That's very kind of you."

The night porter shuffled into the bar, and Wilson followed him, sat on one of the faded red bar stools while the little man unlocked the shutter and let himself in behind the bar.

"What do you wish for, sir?"

Now there's a question, Wilson thought, but he stopped thinking about that when he realised that he didn't have any answer. "Gin and tonic, please. Large one. Half a bottle of the tonic in, ice and lime please."

"Any particular gin, sir?"

"Hendricks if you've got it."

"Wise choice, sir."

The night porter didn't seem in any hurry for Wilson to take the drink up to his room. He sat behind the bar, patient and quiet, looking at nothing in particular, no hurry to be anywhere else. Wilson took advantage of it, because if he took his drink up to his room he would not get a second one.

"So, how long have you been night porter here?"

The old man thought for a moment. "Some time," he said in the end. Wilson sat and drank his drink and then the next, and the night porter sat and did nothing in particular, and Wilson envied him these quiet, simple hours, nothing to do but wait until someone asked you for something, and then you just did it.

He only had two doubles, but he must have been more tired than he thought. When he walked up to the second landing and pushed the fire door open, the first room was numbered 290, but he knew that when he arrived, he had only passed a few doors to get to 210. Wilson followed the corridor round a corner, and then another, and he tried not to look at the carpet because his eyes were tired, and the way the lines seemed to flicker and move made him feel ill. Wilson turned a corner, and there was 210, and the fire door at the end of his corridor.

He looked back, shrugged, fumbled with the key in the lock, and then he was in and for once, he slept.

~

The client presentation went about as well as they always did, which was not particularly well, but not particularly badly either. If they ever did go particularly badly Wilson knew that he would probably be out of a job, and wasn't at all sure what he would do then. The clients were dull but inoffensive, which was a relief as he was there for a week, and he didn't like it if the people were friendly and interesting because the project would end and he would move on to another hotel in another city and he wouldn't see them again but would think how things might have been if it had been otherwise.

Wilson spent most of the evening writing up his notes and preparing a PowerPoint for the next day. He wandered down to the bar partway through the evening and ate a meal of fajitas and chips because he felt more comfortable sitting alone there than he did in the restaurant. He had a gin and tonic before his meal and two with. He contemplated a fourth but the bar was noisy and buzzing with people who knew each other and were having pleasant conversations so he retreated to his room alone and paraphrased things he didn't much care about into one-line bullet points.

When he couldn't focus on the words any more, he got ready for bed and lay down, lost in the wide expanse of the hotel bed. He tried first both pillows, then one, then none, never comfortable. His eyes grew heavy and he tried to will himself to sink into the darkness, hoping that sleep for once would steal in and catch him unawares. Then he opened his eyes wide, jolted into wakefulness by a loud hissing, like steam escaping from a pipe in a film about a damaged submarine.

"What the hell?" Wilson thought. He would say something in the morning if the heating system was this loud. He pulled the blankets up around his head, trying to recapture the moment, but it was too late. He threw back the covers with disgust, swung his legs over the side of the bed, stumbled over to the radiator. Wilson banged it with the flat of his hand then paused, listened, knelt and put his ear to it. Wherever the hissing was coming from, it wasn't coming from there. It sounded as if it were coming from all around the room. Wilson stood up, and the sound stopped, and for a moment the silence sounded louder than the hissing had done.

"Typical," he said in the end, to break the silence as much as anything else, and he walked back toward the bed, then paused. He knew that getting back into bed now would see hours of restless shifting in tangles of sweaty sheets, trying to will himself to sleep but failing, always failing.

He got dressed, and headed for the stairs.

The night porter was behind the desk again. Maybe he would be annoyed at Wilson coming down every night, but if anything the night before he had seemed glad of the company.

"Hello again," Wilson said.

The night porter looked up at him blankly. "Good evening, sir."

Wilson worried that he had judged it wrong. The man

did not seem pleased to see him at all. But he didn't seem displeased either. Just passive, as if they hadn't ever met. "Can't sleep again," Wilson said. "A curse, wish it was otherwise. But tonight – did you hear that hissing?"

"I'm sorry to hear that sir. And no sir, no hissing."

"Oh. Thought it was the heating."

"Would you like me to get someone to have a look at your room tomorrow, sir?"

"No, no. Wouldn't want to put anyone to any trouble. Unless it comes back. Then, maybe... look, I don't want to be a pain, but I wondered if you wouldn't mind... like last night?"

The night porter stared up at him.

"The bar?" Wilson nodded his head towards it, as if the man needed reminding of where it was.

"You'd like a drink, sir."

"Oh, yes, please," Wilson said.

"Of course." The night porter got up and shuffled into the bar, and Wilson followed him, sat on the same faded red bar stool as the night before, while the man unlocked the shutter and let himself behind the bar.

"What would you like to drink, sir?"

"Oh, the same please."

The night porter turned, expressionless.

"Gin and tonic, please," Wilson said, feeling hurt, even if it was just a small thing. Life was a painful succession of small things, and he often thought that was harder than one large thing, but if you tried to tell anyone they would think you were pathetic. "Large one. Half a tonic in it, ice and lime."

"Certainly, sir. Any particular gin?"

"Hendricks," Wilson said, and then he thought that the annoyance might have come through in his voice, and he felt embarrassed for himself. "Please."

"Of course, sir."

Wilson sat and drank while the night porter busied himself behind the bar, tidying and cleaning things that did not appear to need tidying or cleaning.

"Quiet at this time of night," Wilson said, at one point.

"Always is sir," the night porter said. "One of the pleasures of the job."

Wilson stared into his glass. Were there any pleasures in his job? He didn't think so.

The days and the nights passed, as they did. He did his work, and he did it well, and he ate lonely meals and he wandered downstairs in the silent empty hours and drank gin at the bar while the night porter sat and waited. The third night he went down, the night porter got up without a word, opened up the bar, and poured a Hendricks and half the tonic from the bottle, ice and lime. On the fourth night he sat behind reception and again acted as if he had never seen Wilson before in his life. Wilson gave up caring whether it mattered or not. Perhaps the man had memory problems. Perhaps it was his way of entertaining himself in the long, lonely hours.

On his last night in the hotel, Wilson twice stopped writing his final report because he was disturbed by running footsteps in the corridor outside. The second time, he ran to the door of his room and looked out of the spyhole but he was too late and the corridor was empty. Wilson returned to the report. He would deliver it to the client in the morning, and then catch an over-crowded, over-heated train home to an empty flat and a long weekend of not very much in particular.

"Enough," he said to himself, and snapped the laptop shut. He'd get up early and finish it off. Or maybe he'd just hand it over unfinished, they'd probably never read it to the end anyway. He knew he wouldn't do that though, knew that it wouldn't sit well with the vague sense of duty he felt towards everything even though it was never reciprocated.

Wilson let himself out of his room, walked his corridor without looking at the carpet, and took the stairs down to the lobby.

"Good evening sir. Large Hendricks, half a bottle of tonic, ice and lime?" the night porter said.

"You remember me," Wilson said.

"Of course sir, I had the pleasure of serving you when I was last on shift."

"Last night," Wilson said.

"No sir, I wasn't on shift last night."

Wilson thought of a dozen things to say, but didn't see that any of them would make any difference. The little man with the grey, unruly hair got up and ushered Wilson through to the bar.

"You sure this is no bother to you?" Wilson said when his first drink arrived.

"No bother at all, sir."

"I envy you," Wilson said when the second drink arrived, and it came out before he'd even realised he was saying it.

"There are worse ways to spend your life, sir."

Wilson nodded so hard it almost gave him a headache, and told the night porter about some of the little things that made his life a worse way to spend it.

After his fourth, Wilson raised a shaky glass. "To you," he said. Then, without really knowing why, "and to all the other night porters."

"Thank you sir."

"God," Wilson said. "I'm drunker than we thought. I thought, I mean, I thought. Not you. Though you probably did. Oh, I fear I'm making a fool of myself tonight. So sorry. Didn't mean to burden you with all this."

"Not a problem, sir," the night porter said. "It's what I'm here for, sir. Let me help you. Can I help you?"

"Please," Wilson said, and he wasn't quite sure any more what question he was replying to.

The night porter came around to the front of the bar, and eased Wilson off his stool, took his arm and steered him across the bar, to a door at the back.

"Oh, I don't think this is the way," Wilson said.

"Yes sir," the night porter said. "It very much is."

~

Brice rolled out of the taxi and into the hotel. The conference dinner had gone exactly as planned. He'd done all the arse-kissing he needed to do over drinks and canapés, and then he sat down for dinner and expressed surprise and delight to find Helen from the Sheffield office sat next to him. It wasn't that much of a surprise, given that he'd sneaked into the restaurant early and swapped the name cards around on the dinner tables. He worked the Brice charm on Helen for the rest of the evening, apart from a quick few minutes when he dodged out to phone to say good night to the kids and tell Mary how much he missed her. All his effort had struck gold: he had a promise from Helen for dinner the next night, but no conference round table, no annoying geeks from accounts butting in to the conversation. Just the two of them, somewhere else.

He headed for the lift, but then thought twice, and walked back to the lobby to find the night porter. God, Brice thought, most tedious job in the world; you knew all the best places to go but never got to go to any of them. A small man sat behind the reception counter, in some kind of maroon uniform jacket. He had wavy grey hair, which would be unruly if he let it grow any further.

"Need a recommendation," Brice said, "for a nearby restaurant. Nice place, sort of place you'd take a lady." Well, not you, obviously. Sort of place I'd take a lady, he thought, and close at hand enough that's it's just a short walk back to my hotel.

The night porter looked up, looked troubled.

"I'm sorry..." he said.

"You must know somewhere," Brice said. "Come on."

A door opened behind the night porter and a very tall man slid through the door as if he were on rails. "Good evening sir," he said, "I'm the general manager. Welcome to the Hyde Hotel. I'm sorry, our night porter's new. Let me help you - I know just the place. Lovely little restaurant. Perfect for your needs." And he smiled a wide smile that made Brice feel quite uneasy.

Iain Rowan

Tick Box

It was a last minute job but then they often were. He'd booked the room himself, using one of the several identities he had on rotation. He had a strict policy of no more than three uses per name. Edwards had booked the hotel online and used a midweek voucher to get fifteen pounds off his room. That had made him smile. The more money in his pocket the better these days. The hotel's website had said they catered for everything from "the quietest weekend to the wildest of nights". Edwards was hoping for something entirely mundane.

The TripAdvisor reviews he had read of the hotel online all seemed to agree on one thing – the word 'nondescript'. Edwards noted to his amusement that the word also seemed to apply to the staff: the receptionist greeted him with a smile as bland as the hotel décor. Her smile barely stretched to the corners of her mouth and ventured nowhere near her pale green eyes.

"Good afternoon sir," the receptionist greeted him, extending a pale thin hand before she waited for his response. "Can I have your booking confirmation please?"

She had some sort of European accent that he couldn't place. Edwards reached into the pocket of his holdall and pulled out the clear plastic folder which held his booking confirmation, fake passport and corresponding driving licence as well as his spending money for the trip. He handed over the piece of paper with a word of thanks.

The receptionist studied it before clattering away at the grubby grey keyboard in front of her. She frowned at the display on the old fashioned monitor before her pale features softened and she turned back to him.

"Sorry for the delay sir. So we have a double room booked for you at the midweek saver rate of £45."

"That's the one." Edwards smiled.

"Excellent. So Mr…" she paused and looked at the screen before continuing "Stevenson. If you could just sign this document for me confirming your midweek price I'll fetch your room key. Please be aware anything you buy from the minibar will be charged to your card on checkout."

"No problem."

She clattered the mouse before the ancient printer on the desk juddered into life. After a few seconds of droning it spat out a document, which she handed to him. Edwards fished a pen out of his bag and flipped through the pages to where he had to sign. His hand paused above the dotted line as he struggled to remember what the signature looked like on Stevenson's passport. He settled for printing OWEN STEVENSON and handing the paper back. He had briefly considered adding a flourish to the signature but his confidence, still badly shot, reigned in the temptation. Anything that minimised attention and communication with others right now was the best option.

"Thank you Mr…" She had another bored look at the screen, "Stevenson".

She produced a pair of battered electronic key cards from beneath the desk.

"If you head through the double doors," Edwards turned to follow the line of her arm, "and turn right, your room is on the third floor. Lifts and stairs are both through there. If there is any other service that you require, you can dial 0 from your room phone to contact reception. It is manned 24 hours a day."

Out came the narrow, bland grin again as she turned back to her monitor.

"Actually there is one thing please," he said.

She bristled as he spoke and he momentarily saw a flash of annoyance in her eyes as they were bathed in the fluorescent green light of the screen. Her face became immediately placid as she turned back towards him.

"Can I have an alarm call at 7am? You know, I have an early start and all that. I'm not here on holiday after all."

He was overcompensating. The small of his back felt damp.

Bristol...

"Many of our guests are here on business. Not a problem sir," she replied hitting the keys noisily.

He mumbled a brief thank you and turned to leave. He felt her eyes boring into him as he walked towards the stairwell. Yet when he turned to look back at her, she was out of her chair and leaving the reception area through a door behind her desk.

~

His room was as plain as the lobby. The first thing he did was open the window. The frame shrieked as he pushed it open. It opened wide enough that he could slide the flat of his hand through the gap but there wasn't anywhere near enough air coming in. His Vauxhall Corsa sat in the car park below him, surrounded by more expensive cars. It wasn't that Edwards couldn't afford something like that, it just didn't exactly suit his line of work.

Sighing, he filled the ancient plastic kettle from the bathroom sink. It slowly stuttered into life, filling the room with a dull rumble. The steam discoloured the sickly cream wallpaper. There was a big old television in one corner. It had no remote and he didn't bother turning it on. He doubted he would be able to get any Wi-Fi on his laptop, none of the technology he had seen in the hotel so far looked any less than fifteen years old.

Sipping his tea from a jaundiced cup he settled his back against the headboard of the bed, and tried not to picture the thousands of illicit fucks that had been perpetrated on the mattress beneath him. Shifting his weight on the creaking bed, Edwards did his best to make himself comfortable. His back throbbed and ached, the thin pillows propped behind him offered no more comfort than the thick wooden headboard. The tea tasted bitter and hurt his back teeth as he slowly sipped it, using the repetitive motion to calm his ragged breathing. After eighteen months out of the game, it was time to earn some money again.

~

Every job was meticulously planned. Even the urgent ones. Especially the urgent ones. Edwards never left anything to chance in his preparation. Before he had left home he had run through the list of essential items for every job. All eventualities were planned for, his years of experience dictating his preparation. At home, he had a laminated copy of his list pinned to the back of his office door. There was also a spare list in his black Adidas holdall, despite the fact that he could recite the list by heart.

As he knelt by the bag on the floor, he ticked off the items as he saw them.

- Plastic zip ties x10
- Clear plastic tarpaulin x4
- Small black bag containing – one cleaver, two scalpels, one hooked metal dental claw
- Canister of Sevoflurane gas and attached face-mask
- Telescopic 'police-style' truncheon
- Rock hammer
- Surgical gloves
- Electrical tape
- Asthma inhaler (personal use)

From the bag he removed a small Glock 17 and checked the attached silencer. As ever, it was loaded. He cocked it and put it in the back waistband of his tracksuit bottoms. The dull weight against the small of his back reassured him. He hadn't fired the gun for three years, yet it was his constant companion. His solace on every job.

Content that the bag was appropriately packed, Edwards grabbed his car keys and shuffled from the room out into the dingy corridor. As he locked the door, the resident of the room opposite was also leaving his room.

"Hi" said the man, his green tie dazzling against his dull grey suit and pallid skin.

"Hi," replied Edwards, feeling the man's eyes up his tracksuit bottoms.

The two men walked in step down the dimly lit corridor.

"Wish I was off to the gym, always a great way to de-stress isn't it?"

Edwards smiled as they began to descend the stairs.

"Oh without a doubt. Gets rid of that nine-to-five angst."

The suited man smiled his approval. Edwards could still feel the man staring at the side of his face as they walked. He resisted the temptation to talk, just to fill the silence, on the stairs, the suited man held the door open for Edwards.

"Enjoy your gym session pal, try not to put it all back on in the bar later." The suited man said with a smile.

"I'll try. Enjoy your..." his words died off as the suited man strode over to the reception desk, already beaming at the receptionist. "Whatever" continued Edwards to no one but himself.

Edwards stood and watched the man chatting with the receptionist, her pale eyes showing an engagement that had been completely lacking when she had spoken to him earlier. The bland woman looked up and caught him staring over. Porcelain skin on her neck flushed like spilt wine as their eyes met. Leaning on the counter, the suited man cocked his head to look at Edwards, his eyebrows flickering upwards before he turned back to the receptionist.

By the time he reached the car park, Edwards was glad of the fresh air.

~

The job was as simple as it was unusual. A cheating spouse had stepped over the line one too many times. Only this time, the client was a woman. The initial contact had taken Edwards by surprise. In twenty years he had only ever dealt with one other woman, and she had pulled the plug at the last minute. In Edwards' experience, jealousy was an exclusively male emotion. Or at least when it came to dishing out the retribution.

He hadn't met the client. Obviously. He never did. Life was simpler that way. Businesses such as his thrived on a clean, efficient profile and word of mouth advertising. Edwards dealt in human waste disposal. When a person had served their purpose, they found their way to his company. One way or another. This had been his life for decades now, his routine business.

His technique had refined over the years, like a band changing their sound as they outgrow the exuberance of their youth. His violent, messy and enjoyable kills had long since passed. His bloodlust had fallen away over time, dulled by volume and routine. All that mattered now was the pay check. And the drink.

A fast, efficient kill was what he aimed for, more often than not. The violence of his past repulsed him when he thought about it. Everything had changed in Bristol. He felt as though his past was someone else's. A dream he had that no matter how much he thought about it, he couldn't fall back into. He started the car.

~

Edwards parked up two streets over from the address. He had done a quick reccy on the way to the hotel and coupled that with what he had gleaned the night before on Google Maps. He knew exactly what to expect. The keys to the property sang in his pocket as he touched them. A shrill metallic jingle.

He popped some gum into his mouth. Bubble Mint. Chewing slowly and calmly, Edwards distracted his brain from the pummelling his heart was giving his ribs. The kill itself never made him nervous. It had always been the prep. It was why he needed his lists and his maps and directions. They had reassured him back when he was still green. They weren't getting the job done now. When he pulled his hands off the steering wheel, they left greasy damp marks on the black surface. He could feel his left eye twitching as he glanced in the rear view mirror and saw Derek's white van approaching. He wound the window down and felt the cold air chill his lower back and forehead. He wiped his mouth and his forehead with the back of his hand. It was time.

~

By the time he realised Derek had arrived at the back door, the kitchen was in contrast. It had taken him over an hour to redecorate it, much longer than anticipated. The pale cream cupboards and deep, grey granite sideboards were pristine, glistening with a sheen only a professional cleaner could give them. Kneeling on the floor, Edwards jerked his head upwards in surprise. He was vermillion. He was red. For a moment back there, he was lost. On the cusp of being gone forever.

His breath was coming too quickly. A savage tearing at his throat. It sounded as ragged and as bestial as his thoughts had been. Derek's face slipped momentarily from the mask he normally wore in these situations. There was revulsion there, Edwards hadn't seen that in a long time but Derek's face lacked the fear it used to hold. Now he just looked like he wanted to be sick.

Standing up, Edwards let the rock hammer fall from his grasp. There was a muffled thud and a rustle as it came to rest on the tarp beside him. When he looked down, he took a step backwards away from his work, resting one gloved hand on the sideboard. It left a slippery red smear.

"The maid isn't going to be happy with that," said Derek. His face once again stony.

Edwards wasn't sure if he meant the couple's maid or if he was referring to himself. He smiled weakly.

"Sorry," said Edwards, trying to wipe the blood off the sideboard with his hand. He made it worse.

"What have I told you about that?"

"Yeah. I'm rusty." Edwards looked Derek in the eye, until Derek turned his face to the body on the floor. He breathed out slowly, trying to relax his tensed muscles. Wanting to say more, he let the silence wash over him until Derek broke it.

"You've created your own Sistine Chapel here. This is quite the work of art. I mean, I've seen you go postal before but..." he mouthed the word "wow".

Edwards shifted his weight from foot to foot. A few years ago, before Bristol, they would have laughed about this. They would have drank all night and smoked themselves hoarse, never looking each other in the eye as they talked about all the crimes they had gotten away with as if they were the latest episode in some TV show they enjoyed. Not now.

"Pass me that inhaler there Del," said Edwards motioning at his bag. Derek flipped it over to him underarm. Edwards nodded gratefully as he took a few long pulls, feeling it soothe his lungs.

For once he had fastened the tarps well to the bottom of the cupboards. They created a well into the middle of the room where the husband lay on his back. His arms awkwardly arranged and stiffening where they lay. Claret detailed the creases and folds in the tarp. Blood lay pooled in the centre around the body. It had drenched the knees of Edwards' forensics suit. It dripped down now as he stood up. The husband's face was devastated. An unrecognisable atrocity. He would be impossible to identify. His face had crumpled under the blows from the hammer. The resistance of bone slowly giving in as his face caved into a single bloody maw.

It had been the nerves. Or so he told himself. Everything had gone wrong. The husband had already been at home as he let himself into the back door. The element of surprise had been lost just after he had been able to set up the tarps. He'd had to overpower the man as he burst into the kitchen swinging a heavy glass ashtray in front of him. Edwards hadn't had to overpower anyone for nearly a decade. The technique that he had developed, and refined with Derek's help, had held up all this time. By the time the man had succumbed, Edwards thought he was going to outlive the man by a matter of minutes. His chest had constricted tightly, he felt as though his organs were all being squashed together into some sort of paste. His heart still thrummed in his chest even now. His shoulders and lower back nagged at him incessantly. He couldn't let himself forget the swelling on his face and neck, he opened and closed his jaw, checking his teeth. But he had won.

"Looks like it'll be a late one then," said Derek, beginning to unpack his forensics kit. Many of the bottles and packets still had the Cheshire Police logo on them. Memoirs of a former life.

"Yeah, looks like I've made you earn that pay rise pal."

This time, Derek didn't look away. Edwards was unsure if it was the mention of money or the use of the word pal, which had done it but either way he had hit the mark. All the months of phone calls and texts and taunts and threats came back to him as he smiled at Derek. This was the life that Derek had chosen, let him earn it.

"I'd better be off. Stick to the usual timeframe and all that," he said, moving to pack his holdall.

"Leave that here for me. There's blood on the bag, the hammer is a mess and lets be honest, we both know who has the skills in the 'cleaning' field don't we?" It was Derek's turn to smile. Edwards hoped his smirk had been more cutting. "Go on, I'll drop it round in the week."

"Cheers," said Edwards, wearily stepping onto the edge of the tarp. "I appreciate that."

Derek nodded as he stepped past him to get on with the job. Edwards stripped off his forensic suit and ditched it on the side of the tarps. Pulling on another pair of latex gloves, he examined his clothing, dusting at his knees. They looked fine. He stepped out into the back garden and closed the door behind him. He had done it. He was back in business.

~

When he made it back to the Hyde, all Edwards wanted to do was go to sleep, yet it seemed the guests had other ideas. Having left the hotel a half-occupied husk earlier in the day, now in the early evening it had come alive. The car park was full of a wide range of cars, from innocuous hatchbacks like his own to upmarket Jaguars and even a Bentley, parked in a disabled bay right by the door. The lobby was full of energy, the receptionist stood talking animatedly to a number of men wearing suits, handing out keycards and instructions. Her eyes were alive as she laughed and joked with them. Behind him a man in tattered jeans with long dank hair stumbled past on his way to the stairs; not a single other person in the room seemed to notice him.

As he reached his room, he heard the door behind him open. He spun round to see the suited man he had been speaking to earlier that day.

"Ah-ha so we meet again," said the suited man with grin. "Didn't exactly get chance to introduce myself before, I'm David Timms. Here on business this week, how was the gym?"

Edwards took a step back and reached for the man's

hand as he offered it. The proximity of the man's face to his own made him want to swing for him, but he took a breath. "I'm Owen Stevenson. Just up here taking care of a few bits and pieces this week. You know, family stuff."

"Yes, yes of course," replied Timms with a tone that suggested he had no comprehension of what Edwards was saying. "Well I just thought I'd pop out and say hi when you came back from the... gym." His eyes searched for Edwards' holdall but came up empty.

"Yeah, big session. Decided to just leave it all in a locker for tomorrow," said Edwards.

"Of course, of course. Well anyway, our company has had a big win this week and me and most of the sales team are staying here tonight to celebrate. Bit of a naughty one on a school night but we thought we'd put the company credit card behind the bar and make a night of it. Bit of fun, lots of drinks, bit of sport." He gave Edwards an over exaggerated wink as if to welcome him into what he was planning.

"Sounds great, I hope you have fun but I've had a long day, I could do with–"

Timms cut him off. "Well yes of course, have a nap and then get your arse down to the bar for a couple. We've asked everyone in the hotel. I'm sure we can rustle up a nice bit of fanny for a gym bunny such as yourself. Free beer?" His voice had an inflection at the end that made Edwards want to throttle him with his sharp green tie.

"Well I guess I can't say no to a free beer," said Edwards trying to ignore the memories of Bristol that nagged at the base of his brain as he spoke, "I'll be there in an hour or so."

"Brilliant. I knew you would be. See you down there," said Timms and he half jogged down the corridor.

"Yeah. Thanks," said Edwards, letting himself into his room.

~

He was determined that he wasn't going. After a long shower and another cup of mediocre tea, he found himself getting up to turn the television on. The red standby light blinked on and off when he pressed the button but it stubbornly refused to turn on. Edwards looked through the other items he had brought with him and found nothing more entertaining than a change of jeans, not even an old newspaper.

The longer he sat on the bed, the more his body began to tell him to leave. The bed was uncomfortable, that was certain, but something else nagged at him, making him unable to settle in the silent room. Around him the hotel was a hub of noise and activity. Doors slammed and people shouted down the corridor. Below the general hum of noise he could hear a couple having sex loudly somewhere on his floor. He wouldn't have been surprised if it was Timms getting his end away; Edwards reasoned that men like him always did but felt his cock stiffen at the thought of similar opportunities downstairs.

Rooting through his clothes bag, Edwards pulled out a shirt smart enough to pass for a few drinks in a dingy hotel bar and a clean pair of jeans. As he changed out of his clothes, he paused, listening to the noise outside. It was as if the hotel was holding its breath, waiting on his decision. Standing still, Edwards listened as the noise level gradually rose back to its prior volume and he dressed himself quickly and carefully. Snatching up his keycard and his wallet, Edwards pulled the door shut with a click behind him, suddenly thankful to be outside among other people.

~

Timms had been truthful about the beer, at least that was free but three hours and several pints into what had been described as a party, Edwards couldn't honestly say he was having a good time. A swarm of suits crowded around the bar, handing beer out to anyone who approached, regardless of what was actually ordered. Timms was amongst them and other than a quick curt nod to Edwards, he had stayed within his sharply dressed pack all night, laughing and joking too loudly for Edwards' liking.

Starting on his eighth pint, Edwards felt his old pride returning. He was sharing a table with two other men, both of whom were deep in the kind of conversation that only occurred after too much to drink. Pint glass philosophers, Edwards used to call them. But Edwards had never gone in for all that. He liked a scrap when he'd had a drink and right now, he wanted blood. Taking a large swig of beer, he lurched out of his chair and onto his feet. The room swung around him and then steadied itself. He put a hand on the table to steady himself, the group of suited men by the bar came into focus. His prey. Edwards had spent years of his life wiping people like them off the face of this earth and here they were, lauding their money and their privilege and their success. He worked as hard as them, he got his hands dirty. Why should they enjoy it and he had to hide?

"Fuck you!" His voice rang loudly in the crowded bar. Only a handful of people turned to look at him as his words were equally matched by conversation and music. Grasping clumsily, Edwards found his half full pint glass and flung at as hard as he could at the wall, glass exploded, showering the two men sharing his table in sharp fragments. "Fuck you!" he shouted again, this time to his audience.

At the bar, Edwards could see Timms turn and whisper something behind the back of his hand, firstly to one of his colleagues and then to the barman who grinned at him before disappearing through a doorway next to the rows of optics behind the bar.

"You don't deserve any of this shit, the fucking lot of you!" Edwards continued, "You're fucking leeches, parasites you–"

He was interrupted by strong hands behind him as they wrenched his arms up his back and smashed their knees into the back of his, making his legs bend and wobble beneath his weight. Edwards twisted, trying to make eyes with his assailants, he didn't remember the hotel having bouncers on the bar but he struggled against them all the same. His feet slid over the carpet, his jeans damp with beer chafed his leg as he was dragged from the room. Despite his struggles Edwards was held tight and half carried, half dragged from the bar. At the end of the corridor, the barman stood waiting for them to pass. As they drew level with him, he leaned in close to

Edwards ear. The man's breath smelled sour, of days of unbrushed teeth and stale food.

"That was quite the performance sir, almost reminds me of Bristol," he whispered.

Swinging his head violently to look at the man, to see him, to head-butt him, to abuse him, Edwards felt strong hands hold his head still as the plastic face-mask slid over his mouth and nose. Condensation rose in the mask as he tried to calm his breathing, but already his eyes were drooping closed and his limbs were becoming leaden. He was aware of the arms holding him letting go as he slumped to his knees, the deep red carpet with the strange pattern rushing up at him but his eyes closed before the impact and everything became black.

~

When he woke he was kneeling on the floor, his back bent awkwardly over his legs. His hangover had already kicked in yet he felt as though he could only have been out for ten minutes. The top of his head beat a tribal rhythm that the rest of his brain couldn't understand. He moaned softly as the bright spotlights in the kitchen seared his eyes. Without seeing them he was aware of a number of people around him. It took a few moments of squinting for the detail of the room to come into focus; he tried to wipe the water from his eyes but found his hands tied tightly behind his back. The room was brilliant white, scrubbed efficiently clean and it gleamed in the cold bright light from the spotlights. Two men stood in front of him. The barman was wearing a forensics suit as was Timms; laid out on the metal bench next to them was a variety of tools, not unlike his own that he kept so diligently on his lists at home.

"Thanks for joining us Edwards," said the barman. His build and demeanour didn't suit a his deep voice. Next to him, Timms tittered nervously, like a schoolgirl at a disco. Edwards stayed silent. "It's been a while since we've had a guest quite as *prolific* as yourself."

"What the fuck are you on about?" Edwards spat onto the floor; he could taste rubber and plastic from the face-mask.

"The killings of course. The scores of murders you've been committing for decades. Did you think you'd gone under the radar? You underestimate us. We here at the Hyde are your competition."

"My competition? You don't know shit about me."

"We know everything about you Edwards. We know this is your first time in this city and we know for an absolute fact that it wasn't a coincidence that you are in this hotel tonight. And we knew for certain that you couldn't turn down a free beer. We've heard from a reliable source that you can't always resist making a show of your ill-gotten gains."

Edwards heard the clatter of footsteps and half turned, but he heard Derek's voice before he saw his face.

"Should have hung it up after Bristol *pal*. I did suggest it but since when did what I say ever have any bearing?"

Edwards tried to get to his feet but Derek shoved him down onto his knees on the cold, clean floor. His body ached, the fight earlier replaying in his muscles, draining his energy, sapping his spirit. Derek kicked him in the ribs and turned him over to kneel on his shoulders as he lay gasping on the floor. As their eyes met, Edwards' fate took him over for the first time. Derek had checked out behind his eyes, something that used to be so alive had departed. He thought he had seen it earlier that day, but now he was certain.

"It was always about the fucking money pal. I didn't do this job as your lackey for the kicks, I had a family. I *had* one. I never wanted a fifty-fifty split but I deserved better than what you gave me." He slobbered as he growled the word "derisory". Strong hands banged Edwards head against the floor, until voices interrupted his outburst.

"Leave him Derek. Remember why you are here. This isn't your move."

Derek stepped off him and dusted himself down. He grabbed Edwards' feet and dragged him to the corner of the room that Edwards dimly recognised as a kitchen. One side of the room had been cleared and tarps taped to all of the available surfaces. Derek's MO. Edwards tried to fight but the struggle left him breathless. His senses were still returning from the gassing, with his hands and feet bound he knew he could only fight them off for a matter of minutes before the inevitable. Derek punched him in the face again, his nose loosened with a gristly crunch and he lay back on the tarps with a pronounced rustle.

"Fuck you!" Edwards screamed, his voice dulled by the blood seeping from his nose and down his face.

"You shouldn't be so angry Mr Edwards or Mr Stevenson or Mr Wilson or whichever of your names you use. You've been chosen. Have you ever been to a restaurant and chosen which lobster you'd like to eat? Well this is very much the same thing and Mr Timms here – assuming that is his real name – chose you. Don't you feel special?" asked Tom. The barman's eyes gleamed as he spoke. He clasped his hands excitedly, his latex gloves squeaking together.

"What we are doing here at the Hyde Hotel is a good thing. Timms here is probably going to torture you tonight – I know he is definitely going to murder you. His aggression will be taken out on you, a gun for hire. A worthless sell-sword that nobody, not even his old colleague," he motioned to Derek, "will miss. Isn't that better than him going home and hitting his wife or his children or his lover or a colleague? High pressure jobs bring their own stresses and strains, his performance when he goes back to work will be much improved I'm sure."

Derek leaned in over Edwards. Edwards could taste the bitter taste of blood as it coated his tongue and throat. "Some people will pay through the nose to get away with something this ugly *pal*, just a shame you never realised it. But don't you worry, they're taking care of me now." He pulled himself to his feet and unrolled Edwards' own portfolio of weapons. Timms stepped forward eagerly and took up the rock hammer, testing the weight in his hand. "Oh the irony," leered Derek as Timms stepped forward.

Timms stopped and turned to Derek and the barman. "Thank you Derek and thank you Tom. You really do have no idea how much I needed this."

Edwards tried to struggle to his feet, wrestling his

shoulders and hips from the tarps. The rustling in his ears was deafening and his broken nose throbbed pain rhythmically through his face. He had just about made it to his knees when he caught the sound of the hammer as it circled through the air. Pain blinded him for a split-second before everything went black.

~

When it was over and he had cleaned up, Derek surveyed the room. Fried breakfasts would be cooked here in a matter of hours. A minimal staff would pace about these floors with no idea of what had happened here whilst they slept. He smiled to himself. That's how it had always been, his job had never been fancy or full of glory, he just returned things to their natural, innocuous state so that people could get on with their lives untroubled by the atrocities that they would never experience. And if he had done his job right, atrocities that they would never even suspect.

He walked through the hotel and out into the lobby. Tom was waiting for him there. They shook hands as they watched Timms, dressed immaculately, checking out of the hotel.

"You did some excellent work tonight Derek, this whole thing wouldn't have happened without your input and your knowledge of Edwards. Timms was a really important client and this little venture of ours will really take off now we can break into his circle of friends... and let's face it, why stop there?"

"Not a problem, a fair day's work for a fair day's pay suits me just fine. I knew he would bite on the money saving voucher, people like that always do." They smiled and shook hands, before Tom walked away from him and through the door to the office behind reception.

"I trust everything was to your liking Mr..." the receptionist looked at her screen before continuing, "Timms?"

"Oh yes, everything was spectacular. Thank you. It was everything that I was promised it would be." Timms straightened his tie and smiled. He already felt like a new man, as if a weight had been lifted from his shoulders; his soul felt lighter.

"I'm very glad to hear it sir," replied the receptionist. "Please if you just bear with me a moment, I'll print off a special voucher for you so that you can get fifteen pounds off your next midweek stay with us."

"That would be great, never hurts to save a few quid here and there does it?" replied Timms with a smile.

"Well we do hope to cater for all of customers, whether it's your first stay here or your last," said the receptionist as she handed over the voucher.

"Oh I'll definitely be back soon," said Timms. "Without a doubt."

Derek put his hands in his pockets and began to whistle as he stepped out through the main doors into the early morning mist. He was looking forward to it already.

Dan Howarth

The Edifice of Dust

Listen:

There are five burned sticks, all in a row, thrust deep into cold and barren ground. The field is flat, stretching from one end of the sky to the other, with only hard outcroppings of jagged rock to relieve the eye. Dead dry grass hugs the crumbling soil. The wind is a slashing knife. There are no structures to bar its way; no houses, no huts, no standing stones. Nothing to keep it caged; nothing to keep it tame.

So. The five burned sticks. Sharpened to a point on the edge of a rock, blackened in the heat of a flame, stabbed into the heart of the earth. A strip of white cloth winds around them. Lashed between the sticks with a series of inexpert knots that nevertheless somehow seem to be holding true. The cloth is rough and ragged, and the closer you look at it the more easily you are able to see what it is made of: an intricate mesh of fibres, matted and ingrained with flecks of dirt. The fibres weave and separate, undulating together against the wind. They look like one unit, one organism, but in fact they are many. They are legion. If any one of them were pulled – if any single thread were to come unraveled – the cloth would fall and the sticks would tumble and the wind would hold sway over all.

Five burned sticks in a field. A strip of white cloth.

This, it is believed, was humanity's very first wall.

~

"But how *are* you?" said Chelsea. "I mean really?"

"Oh, you know me," said Phaedra. "Keeping it together."

Phaedra listened into the receiver as her sister struggled to build the proper sentence. The right word on top of the right word, stone by stone and brick by brick. Poor Chelsea. She was an interior designer and knew nothing of construction.

"Everyone misses you," was, at last, all she could offer.

"Oh, I rather doubt that, Chelsea," Phaedra said, leaning on the windowsill and peering out through the smoky glass. All was calm today. A fine haze of fog wafted over the tower-blocks of the city, and a steady drift of cars crept past beneath their shadow.

It made a nice change, every so often, to see into the present.

"Of course they do. I know it's been bad but you can't just up and vanish like that. If you'd at least tell me where you are..."

"It's more a question of *when*," said Phaedra.

"When you want to come back?"

"Sure," said Phaedra. "Why not."

A silence. More bricks atop bricks. "Are you working?"

"No," said Phaedra. "I don't suppose that is what I am doing. If I were working someone would be paying me. If I were working I would be subject to someone else's whim.

Someone else's time." She looked up at the corner of the windowpane. Thin motes of dust had begun to gather around the edges. She swept them away with the flat of her hand. They scattered, unseen, across the carpet.

"I don't suppose this month's *Architectural Digest* has come out yet," she said.

Chelsea rustled uncomfortably. "It has. Do you want me to send you a copy?"

"No need. I have a fairly good idea of what it'll say."

"Listen," bridled Chelsea, "it wasn't just *your* reputation, you know. All the assistants, all the engineers. The investors. Me."

"Ah," said Phaedra, "but you didn't design the place, did you, Chelsea? Wasn't your name on the cheque. Wasn't your hand that drew up the blueprints. A Phaedra Lang Original! Everyone was ever so excited."

"We all fall down sometimes," said Chelsea. "You've just got to get back on the horse."

"I didn't fall from a horse," said Phaedra, distracted by movement at the edge of the room. A small bearded man in doublet and hose had wandered in from the left-hand wall and was trying to navigate some invisible obstacle. Phaedra could see the sweat soiling the collar of his ruff, could hear the creak of the floorboards beneath his cracked leather boots. He smelled of hops and body odour and beef. He gave her an anxious glance; she jerked her head in the direction of the opposite wall; he nodded his thanks and walked through, into the patterned paper.

"Buildings collapse sometimes, Phae," Chelsea was saying. "It happens. It wasn't–"

"Walls. Did I ever tell you about the *first* wall, Chelsea?" said Phaedra, watching the man disappear.

"What?"

"Listen," said Phaedra. "There are five burned sticks, all in a row."

"I know this story," said Chelsea. "This is that speech you gave at the Architectural Association. I've *heard* it."

"Five burned sticks," said Phaedra, "all in a row."

"Phae, listen..."

"Thrust deep into–"

"I have to go," said Chelsea, and hung up.

Phaedra looked at the receiver, weighed it in her hand. "Cold and barren ground," she said, and replaced it in the cradle.

She sat down on the bed and looked around her hotel room. It was, in a certain sense, exactly the way it had always been.

~

She had chosen the hotel because of the name.

The Hyde. It spoke to her. Suggested things. A tough outer skin, impossible to penetrate, designed by Nature to shield. To keep shattered bones and tender meat from suffering any further outrage. To protect from cold, from exposure.

It had possibilities. Possibilities that would not be immediately apparent to any eye not sufficiently trained, as Phaedra's was, to be attuned to them. But she felt them as she entered the lobby, felt them vibrate through the scuffed parquet floor, heard them in the hum of the dim overhead lights as she signed herself over for what the desk clerk termed an "indefinite stay". Her footsteps drowning in thick cheap carpeting as she followed the indifferent bellhop; the sullen strobe of dull light leaking out of the globes studding the corridor; the click of the key and the whine of the door – all these things added up to an understanding, an instinct honed razor-sharp by years of study and observation. She could feel the soil beneath the hotel, black and silent, a thousand feet below.

Her first night was quiet. No one called. No one knew where to call. Back at what she laughingly called her home, the landline screamed night and day, and her mobile was wracked with buzzing tremors. Journalists wanting quotes. Quotas. Tallies of the costs, the damages, the injured. She'd yanked the plug from the landline, drowned the mobile in the pool.

She lay in bed and listened to the Hyde's four walls of silence. Her room lay at the hotel's hollow heart. A single cell in the hive. There was a room buffeting hers on every side. No windows, of course. Hers was a hidden space: chthonic, interstitial. Below and between.

The longer she listened, the deeper she heard. Sound crept in between cracks in the quiet. Voices muffled under plaster. Snatches of talk, of song. Shuffling feet on carpet, on board. On concrete and earth. She flicked on the light and knelt on the bed and pressed her hand to the wall above it. It felt warm, vaguely yielding. Like flesh. Like hide.

Her palm came away coated in dust. She examined it, held it up to the light where it could gleam. One of her teachers at architectural college had said once that dust was made up of dead skin cells; it flaked away from the main structure of the body and went where it would, piling up, gathering. Dust did not, could not, exist in places where no human had ever lived, because dust could not exist unless a human body was there to slowly crumble away to it.

Phaedra called the front desk and requested that the hotel's blueprints be brought to her room. She also requested the strongest vacuum cleaner they had.

The first thing she did, after sucking up every dust particle she could find, was sharpen her pencils and blow the shavings across the blueprint, spread out on the desk before her. She could see her room from here. A god's-eye view. Reading the entrails. She picked up her pencil and sketched in a tiny rectangle on the north side of her room. On the wall. A window.

She had sat back and looked at her work, and found that it was good. She'd turned in her chair and gazed out through her window to the heavy sleet beyond.

The next day she'd called the front desk again and requested every blueprint the hotel had ever had. All the way back to its inception. All the way *past* its inception.

She would open it up and cut it right down to its marrow.

~

That had been some time ago. What time and when, Phaedra couldn't say. Her indefinite stay had become quite definite.

This in itself was, she supposed, unusual. Hotels were by nature unmoored: places you were always leaving, places you had always left. When you moved into a house, you made it your own: you marked your territory, one houseplant and tchotchke and family photo at a time, until the liminality was exorcised and the place took on your character. No one ever stayed in a hotel long enough to lend it their own character; therefore the places were infinitely malleable.

She had now been redesigning the Hyde from the inside out for a fair period of time. It wasn't always the *same* time. She looked out the window. The Great Fire of London raged beyond the glass. The heat looked infernal, the towers of smoke leviathan, but none of it reached her room. It was happening right now, this very minute, but it had also happened long ago, and was long gone. Last night, Phaedra had sketched a priest-hole from 1666 back into the Hyde's modern-day blueprint; she assumed that was why she was seeing this now. Yesterday, it had been a 12th-century monastery in Northumberland, set upon by Vikings. The day before that, New Street in Birmingham, just after the Blitz. And the day before that, leagues of cool grey water, licking at gritty sand and rough, misshapen pebbles.

She stood up and paced the eighteen steps from the bed to the window. Exactly eighteen. The room was comprised of fifteen square metres. One hundred and sixty-one square feet. Thirteen by thirteen. An unlucky number, for some. She could redesign the room, make it bigger, more comfortable. Palatial, even. She had never been tempted to do so.

Phaedra stared out at the billowing flames and sighed. Her breath fogged the glass. That, for now, was real. The air in her lungs, real and here, and now.

She shouldn't have called Chelsea. Chelsea didn't need to know how she was doing. Chelsea didn't need to know she was all right.

If she was all right.

She was all right. Of course she was. She had her freedom, hard-won and uncompromised. No idiot engineers to screw up the purity of her designs; no useless employers to tell her those designs weren't practical; no lazy, irresponsible, incompetent contractors to go half-measures on workmanship and materials. She had no limits now. She was an antibody in a vast organism that survived independent of anything external to itself. She lived outside the flow of time, and nothing could touch her.

A discreet knock. Phaedra waited, crossed the room, and opened the door. A tray of food and drink sat on the threshold, neatly arranged as always. She picked it up and took it inside. She placed it on the desk, on top of the blueprints, and stared at it, rocking back in her chair.

She put it on the floor, next to the other trays, and told herself that this time she would definitely eat it. But later. Later.

She had time.

~

Buildings collapse.

Phaedra turned the words over in her mind as she sat up in bed that night, looking out her window. The moon rose over hard-packed earth and gritty stone, tawny candlelight leaking from lopsided wooden doorways. Hooves clopped. A church bell tolled.

Chelsea was not wrong, in a sense. Buildings did collapse. It was what they wanted to do. They leaned in on themselves, groaning beneath their weight, bent double under the lodestone of their own history, longing to return to rubble and ash. Slaves to entropy. Blood-soaked ziggurats and paved gardens and libraries fattened on human knowledge, sheer cliff-faces of sleek glass and curving metallic lenses that enchained the sun and melted the cars below with their brilliance – all harboured secret desires, perverse and masochistic urges running counter to their own survival. They all wanted to let go.

Phaedra had always been able to sense their vanishing. Even before she was famous, before she was Phaedra Lang Incorporated, when she was a student and nothing and no one, she had felt the ghosts of dead buildings when she walked the city streets. She knew herself well enough to know she couldn't survive outside a city, but the taste of debris lay acrid on her tongue, unnoticed by anyone else, and there were too many lines you had to follow: train lines, tram lines, ley lines, desire lines. Endless branching veins dribbling away to nothing, spilling the buildings' spent life force out into sewer and canal, ditch and forest, soil and root. And she could feel herself, her very own structure, moving towards that same end: little pieces of herself, a dandruff flake here, a snapped fingernail there, coming away, coming apart. At any moment the atoms and molecules that made her up could disband; at any moment, out there in the huge and wide and empty streets, she too could fall to dust and scatter away on the wind.

But that wasn't happening now. The trick was never to allow the structures the release they craved. That was true history, sane history; that was civilisation. What good, after all, was human ingenuity, human effort, if it couldn't keep an edifice standing, couldn't keep one's head above the dust?

No. Much better to remain where she was. Hiding, Hyding, wrapped safe and secure in hide. Better to be the Demiurge, the god in the machine, designing the world from within, than to shed the protective skin and become nothing more than a speck. She'd achieved ephemeralization, Buckminster Fuller's dream: doing "more and more with less and less until you could do everything with nothing". And who in this world had more nothing than she?

Phaedra glanced over at the food. It was starting to rot. The scent of decaying fruit hung in the air, sweetness laced with mould. A skein of dust furred the edges of the plates, the rims of the glasses. It was creeping back in through the cracks.

She threw aside the bedclothes and stood. She crossed the room—twenty-one steps—and hoisted up the stack of trays. She took them to the dumbwaiter, the one from 1937 she'd drawn back in last Tuesday, and tossed them down the shaft. She peered into the dark and watched the china break, the glass splinter; watched the powdered ghosts of her own dead skin as they billowed away.

~

And the dust travelled, and this is what the dust saw:

Reams. Layers. Uncountable strata of black stone. Rings spiralling the innards of a great dead tree. Sticks bound together by the same strip of cloth.

The dust that had been Phaedra Lang waltzed gently through the veins of the Hyde Hotel, all its secret tunnels and traps and curves and curlicues, through the porous membranes of When and Where. It swept through a latticed window on the third floor and down streets of grey cobblestone slick with wet red, hissing gaslight and steaming horse dung and gentlemen who were neither gentle nor, entirely, men. It ground beneath the stacked boot-heels of beautiful young people dancing to hard sounds from hard vinyl, dyed scarves and dyed hair flying in a glossy whirl of panstick and sweat; they stomped it into the next room, where fever-browed Richard Dadd stabbed brush into paper, carving out tangled flowers and mad-eyed, sickly fairies. It drifted through an air vent on the ninth floor and into the baptismal font where sunlight came to drown, where the infant William Blake stared up at cross-hatched wooden beams as water swirled around his soft and unformed skull. It joined hands and partnered with the shed flesh of other architects, Brunel and Brown, Hawksmoor and Wren. Their disintegrated bodies sucked into the black mesh of Joe Meek's microphones and down his flushing toilet, past a river of antique shit and into the noxious quiet of a plague pit, cages of bone and teeth tearing at one another in the sick earth, fighting for space no longer occupied and air no longer breathed; sank into the foundations and drank the blood of sacrifice in high tall grass, watched over by stones that sang the arias of wind and water and sky. And then there was prehistoric snow and huffed breath and warm brown fur, and the floors and mouths of caves, and dirt and rock and silence.

Snow and fur, stone and blood. The dust washed through, and past, and all around and back and forth.

Phaedra slept, in her bed, in her room, in the Hyde, on a patch of ground on a dark and ancient planet. And as she slept the dust gathered, and watched, and settled back comfortably into the home it had never, even for a moment, left.

~

Phaedra awoke to muted chatter and the cloying scent of long-extinguished cigarettes. Two young men in white corsets and red lip-paint sprawled on her bed, one on either side, talking over her and sharing a smoke. One blonde, one brunette. White arsenic and syphilis scars. The molly-house, she remembered, from 1792. She'd sketched its antechamber back in, very late last night, her exhaustion exhilaration, a mind-bending drug. The dust's return had enervated her, electrified her with dread. She'd had to work. She'd had no choice.

She sat up between the men, who ignored her; it wasn't as if she were a paying customer. She couldn't understand anything they said, anyway. The words of the past-visitors were lost forever; when they spoke, all she heard was a high-pitched rush, wind whistling down a chute.

Phaedra sat down at her desk, feeling hung-over. The blueprints spilled off the edge of the table now, the papers taped together as the Hyde's landscape flourished and grew beneath her guiding hand. What had once been doodling in the margins had become a rushing tide of scrawl: page upon page of crammed pencil and frantic ink, buildings and structures butting up against one another in frank disregard for their proper place in space and time. Her plans were, quite literally, unraveling. She sat back in her chair and stared at the ceiling. "'Bedlam and Gehenna,'" she said, "'equal to the New Jerusalem.'" The youths on the bed glanced at her with mild and curious disdain.

"It's all so old," she explained, knowing full well they wouldn't hear her. "Nothing new under the sun. That's what they say, isn't it?"

The brunette looked at the blonde and said something quizzical. The blonde shrugged.

"There's a rather interesting theory I once heard tell of," said Phaedra. "Sort of an occult science, if such a thing isn't a contradiction in terms. It's called megapolisomancy. I wonder if you know it?"

They stared at her.

"No, I thought not," said Phaedra. "Well, essentially, it's the idea that you can use the designs and materials of cities to predict the future. Even to change the future, if you like. It's got something to do with the energies that accumulate. All the detritus. Psychic dust."

She looked around the room. The carpet was becoming obscure. Its pattern submerged beneath clumps, heaps, piles of powder. It could almost be sand. Could almost be a day at the beach.

"I've never found that to be true," she said. "I wish it were. Sometimes I thought I could see the future, just outside my field of vision. When I first started sketching

I had an idea that eventually I'd be able to see it clearly. I'd be able to walk right into it with my hands open and I could reach right out and touch it. But I've never seen the future. Not once. All I see is the past."

Phaedra scrubbed her eyes with her hands. The men waited patiently for her to continue.

"I have a theory of my own," she said. "About that. I think the past *is* the future. It's your present, of course. You're watching me from there right now, and it would never occur to you that this moment, this very instant, is something that is already long gone. But for me, it's the past, and it's just going to keep happening again and again. A Moebius strip. Time doubling back on itself and devouring its own tail."

She stood. "Alternately," she said, "I have never been able to see into the future because I don't have one."

She looked at the dust. "Does that not bother you?" she asked the men, gesturing at it. "Not at all?"

The men blinked, eyes dull with annoyance. The blonde looked at the brunette and said something brief. The brunette threw back his head and laughed for a very long time.

Phaedra watched them, then turned back to her blueprints. She sat down with her pencil in hand and didn't look up again until the sun was down.

~

Sweat curled the hair in front of her eyes and made it hard to see. The plans were a blur of black and blue and the scrape of lead on paper ground in her ears. She looked at the pencil in her hand and was startled to see she had chewed it, a habit she'd believed shed in adolescence. Lead on the page, on her teeth, in her stomach. Perhaps it would ground her. She felt so terribly light.

The blueprints tumbled to the floor, longer and more elaborate now than they had ever been. There were so many rooms, so many floors. The Hyde might go on forever. But of course it already did.

The hand that clutched the bitten pencil had held it so tight the nails had cracked. Her index finger had a hangnail so loose it flapped when she flexed her knuckle. She bit it off and spat it onto the carpet, to join the rest of the waste. Powder rode her gums; she ran her tongue over them and tasted bitterness. She looked down at her palms and saw they sweated dust.

She dived to the floor to retrieve her fingernail. The phone cord tangled around her legs and pulled the receiver into her hands. Chelsea had picked up on the other end before Phaedra had even realised she'd dialled.

"Mm. Hello?"

"What am I made of?" said Phaedra, scrabbling for the nail.

"Phae?" said Chelsea, instantly awake. "Is that you?"

"Maybe. What am I made of, Chelsea? Am I something solid? Am I a well-constructed edifice, designed to last? Am I up to code, do you think?"

Silence. Phaedra spread her hand out over the carpet. The nail had to be someplace. Everything was someplace. But the dust, the dust. There was just so much.

"Phae, please. Come home. Nothing is worth this. Mum's worried. I'm worried."

"You shouldn't worry, Chelsea. If you worry at things too much, they come undone." She thrust her hand into a pile of dust. It collapsed, avalanching across the floor.

"Nobody is angry at you. I can come and get you if you like."

"You don't even know where I am."

"Tell me. Tell me where you are."

"I don't know either," said Phaedra, and shrieked with laughter. The sharp nail stabbed deep into her fingertip. She picked it up between thumb and forefinger and swallowed it down.

Chelsea sounded as if she might be crying. "*Please, Phae.*"

Phaedra wondered if she were crying, too. Her eyes felt heavy. "I think the strip's unwinding, Chelsea. The sticks can't hold."

"I can come to you. I can come right now. Just give me an address. Give me something."

Phaedra rolled onto her back and stared at the ceiling. She rubbed a hand across her eyes. The hand came away coated in dust.

"There's no address," she said. "Nothing is fixed." She sat up. Her fist balled and struck the ground. "Not yet. Not yet."

"Phae," said Chelsea. "Just stop. Stop. Let go."

Phaedra said nothing. She wound the phone cord tight around her leg, tighter, tighter, trapping the blood inside. She looked at it. She moved her foot. The extension tore away from the wall.

~

Shredding paper, shredding plans. Dust-caked fingers ripping blueprints in half. The sound of tearing raked her eardrums.

Phaedra bound herself in her own design. Wound the strips of paper around her bare arms and naked torso, tight enough to hurt but not tight enough to tear. The paper had to remain intact. It had to hold her together. The Hyde's endless floors and uncountable rooms bulged over her abdomen, crackled up her thighs, strangled around her throat. She sweated ink and lead.

She sat on the bed, rocking forward and back, forward and back. She would be bare if not for her plans. Only they kept her from joining the dust.

The dust. It glittered in the air, curling lazily in shafts of cool light. Smoke and ash. The shed skin of the world. Waves of it, hills of it, mountains and peaks of it. It had conquered the carpets and floorboards, the chairs and the tables and wardrobe and desk; had mounted the windowsill and smothered the glass. A great white swell of dunes; an unstoppable towering drift.

The dust had a sound. It whistled and rustled and sang, and it spoke. Its voice was serrated edge, eternal age, rust and earth and fire. Old blood and withered bone.

Phaedra shrank back against the pillows, hugging her knees to her chest, and tried not to listen. She tried not to listen.

She listened.

And the dust spoke, and this is what the dust said:

Come with us. Come with us and let go. Let everything go. Let yourself go.

Phaedra shook her head and burrowed her face into her forearms.

Let yourself go. Let yourself go everywhere. This room is small. This structure is small. You are small but you do not have to be. Keep nothing together. Set it aside. Set it apart. Open your hands. Let yourself go.

Phaedra looked up. Specks danced across the ceiling, converged and diverged and shattered and scattered. Granules of glistening light.

We have seen much, said the dust. *We have seen everything. We have been everything. We have been places. We will take you there.*

Phaedra let out a sob.

Listen. Listen.

She listened.

Listen. We have been places. There are so many places. We will take you there. We will take you to the reliquaries of saints who died before names were born. We will take you to cities washed clean beneath the ocean's chill, crippled geometries drawn up by the light of burned-out stars. We will take you to desert graveyards where jackal-headed men devour the shrunken silk-wrapped bodies of cats. We will take you to the peaks and crags where only birds can breathe, where things of beak and claw circle and mate in temples made from lightning-struck trees and strips of dried flesh. We will take you to towers of broken teeth. We will take you to circles of flower and stone. We will take you to walls of stick and cloth. We will take you to the high places, to the thin places, the weightless places where the earth falls up forever. We will take you to the edifice of dust, which is all the world. Let yourself go and we will take you there. We will take you there. We will take you there if you only let yourself go.

Phaedra listened and listened and listened. She looked at the dust and she looked at the ground and she looked at the ceiling.

She opened her mouth and drew a breath. Drew it all inside.

She held her breath. She held it as long as she could. She was going to breathe out. She could feel it building inside her, feel the oxygen burning in her lungs. She was going to breathe out. Any moment now.

Any moment.

~

The desk clerk looked up from his newspaper.

A vast pale swirl of dust glided across the lobby's checkerboard floor, whirling up to the ceiling, brushing the light fixtures and leaving them to swing. It left traces of itself on the picture frames, the wallpaper, the faded chairs and chipped wooden desk. It spread long fingers across the clerk's face, trailed over and through his hair. He stared, wordless, watching as it passed him by.

The dust swept through the doors and out, all the way out, into whatever lay beyond.

Amelia Mangan

Lost and Found

Sept. 24

Finally arrived. My heart's dancing. There's a slight chill to the air, a perfect greeting. Mist, too, but not like the constant drizzle back home. The streets are busy with people, buses, taxis, nothing unusual. Yet it all feels different, the world going on without me.

I wish the people I work with could see me. They take vacations twice a year, usually to some awful place like Kauai or the Caribbean, where there's nothing to do. They lie around on the beach, and drink too much. Last year some of them took a cruise together. What a nightmare, sailing the Pacific coast with a boatload of your co-workers. Can you imagine?

This is my vacation and I'm doing exactly what I want, for a change. I tried explaining to my supervisor, who stared at me and said, "Oh well, have a good trip, try to get some sun." Stupid woman.

Here I am, at last, in the heart of Muriel Watson's hometown, in the hotel where she spent her childhood, where she honeymooned, where she wrote her novels, and – I'm getting ahead of myself. I'm here. Hard to believe, but it's all real.

The train was full of tourists. I stood in line at the ticket booth while two of my fellow Americans harangued a young woman with blunt, jet streaks of eyeliner and meticulously drawn plum lipstick. She regarded them with the cruel patience of a child conducting an experiment on a pet hamster.

When my turn came I said as little as possible, hoping I might be mistaken for Canadian. The young woman studied the hotel name and address on my itinerary. She looked me over and asked if I knew the area. I said no. She took pity on me and wrote down my connections. She told me to be careful. I mumbled a brief apology for being stupid and told her I didn't know which direction to go, to find the platform. She pointed and I mumbled thanks.

While I waited, standing directly under the sign for the train, feeling the cold rush of air from the tunnels swirl up around my legs, I heard my compatriots again, whining about the lack of customer service. Then they lapsed into what they probably thought to be a funny imitation of the ticket booth woman's accent. No wonder they hate us over here.

The Hyde Hotel is smaller than it appears in the photos online. Not as old as I'd assumed, refurbished many times, according to the front desk clerk.

"The cornices and balustrade are latter day embellishments," he said.

He was a young man who seemed middle aged, rundown or broken somehow. Or am I being arrogant? I don't want to be one of those rotten tourists, accusing everyone of being dour. I have to remember why I'm here, and not become distracted with observations about how *this* is just like home, while *that* is so unlike what I'm used to. Always comparing things to other things.

The clerk didn't blink when he noted my reservation. He reminded me to exchange keys at the front desk each time I trade rooms. (They have actual keys here, not those key cards I despise.)

"Have you signed on for one of the local tours?" he asked.

"No, I'm on my own tour," I said. "Following the haunts of my favourite author."

"Oh?"

"Yes. Muriel Watson."

He frowned. "Sorry, I don't know the name."

"Her parents used to work in this hotel," I said. But he seemed to have lost interest.

I thanked him too many times. Should I have tipped? There was no bellboy, or porter, in sight. Only the clerk, a couple waiting to check in, and an old man dozing on a sofa in the corner. But it didn't matter. I only carry one small suitcase. "Don't pack what you can't hoist or drag by yourself," is my travel motto. Not that I've traveled much. Once to Vancouver. Once to Portland.

Upstairs, the corridors are so narrow I can't imagine two people walking side-by-side. Stepping out of the nausea-inducing "lift," which took off like a rocket and immediately slowed to a grinding halt on the third floor, I nearly fell over making the first turn toward my room. The hallway is curved, which seems odd in a building that looks square. Optical illusion, or an architectural compensation.

I found the room right away, 309. I stood staring at the number until I heard the elevator again. It's silly to be so excited. But I've come a long way on this adventure. I want to savour all of it. In fact, I wanted to take a picture, but I've lost my phone. (I used the lobby telephone to report it missing and cancel the service until I get home.)

The room is larger than I expected but also simpler, and less attractive. A narrow bed with pinstriped sheets and matching quilt. A nightstand with a lamp. One straight-backed chair and a small table next to the window. The view is a rooftop with water stains and pigeon feathers, on the other side of an alley. I try to imagine Muriel Watson spending her honeymoon here and the thought makes me melancholy. Maybe the view was different in the early '60s. Maybe there was a garden next door. I don't know. The biography doesn't say.

I'm feeling very tired. Plane, train, bus. I was hungry earlier but now I only feel fatigue and that wave of something like sorrow. Chalking it up to too much distance covered in one day.

I've peeled the covers off the bed and I plan to rest for half an hour or so. Then I'll see what's available from room service.

~

Sept. 25

Didn't know where I was when I woke up a little while ago. Thought I was still traveling. The rapid compression of places, names, faces I'll never see again. I replayed my journey while sleeping. Train stations beneath buildings marked with scaffolding and tarp. Above-ground platforms, a distant whistle, vaulted canopies of rainclouds. A blank ticket in my hand. Trying to remember the name of my destination.

The sheets are damp with sweat. They don't smell like me, probably a composite of strange food and chemical and mineral differences in the water across regions. The bed felt fresh and crisp, when I lay down. I'll have to remember to leave the housekeeping sign on the doorknob. Otherwise, my 'privacy will be respected,' according to the hotel greeting card.

Oddly enough, I'm not at all hungry. Although I've missed the complimentary breakfast. I'll shower before I go out, and find a place for lunch while I'm exploring the neighbourhood. On my first tour I'll track down Philips's, the bookstore where Muriel Watson gave the only reading of her all-too-brief career.

Can't help staring at the ceiling and wondering if the crumbling plaster was the same, when she spent her honeymoon here. Or on countless occasions when she must have played games as a child, when her parents worked at the hotel. Did she hide in the rooms and stairwells, and jump out to startle the maids? Her biography doesn't say so, but it's a slender volume. One hundred and ten pages to convey a writer's life. If her books had been more popular, if her themes had been more universal, if she had nurtured the will to promote her work, or if she had won any of the prizes for which her books were nominated, the desk clerk might have known her name. But then she wouldn't be mine, all but forgotten by the writers' clubs and organisations to which she belonged. Her dark hair and pale gray eyes luminous in the photo on the back of her books. Slim fingers arched elegantly around a cigarette. Lips drawn into a sort of smile, a resigned smirk.

I like to imagine young Muriel chasing shadows through a sun-dappled lobby. I like to think she was happy here, once. As a child, and maybe as a young woman. Despite the sad failure of her marriage to an aspiring poet named Timothy Davies, who shared this room with her so many years ago. Davies the Disappointed, who fled the marriage bed and returned to a bedsit in Islington.

Morbid today, probably the result of too much travel and, now, too much sleep. Shower, then lunch.

~

Sept 25

Before leaving the hotel, I stopped at the front desk. My intention was to check my directions to the bookshop on Merton Lane and make sure my room change is scheduled for tomorrow morning.

Everything looked more shabby than I remembered. I must have been exhausted yesterday, not to notice the threadbare sofas and carpet. I expected the lobby to be busy. Or, I don't know what I expected. In any case, there were only two people, both elderly men wearing business suits, seated facing one another in armchairs, reading newspapers.

The same clerk at the desk as yesterday nodded as I approached, and listened politely to my questions.

"We have you booked into 219 for one day, following your stay in—"

He consulted a computer screen without typing anything and it occurred to me that the hotel was small enough to appear on a simple grid. "—309. Your key will be provided at check-in. Will you need assistance?"

"No," I said. "No, thank you. I wonder if you can tell me, which way should I start out, to find Merton Lane?"

He studied my face for a split second, and turned toward the glass double doors at the north end of the lobby. He pointed but I couldn't tell in which direction.

"Is that left?" I asked.

"Left would be the longer route. Should you decide to take in the sights along the main road, you will end up at the market."

He didn't offer any further advice. I didn't want to waste his time. After all, I have a map.

I'm still a little confused, and embarrassed, about what happened next.

The way the desk clerk said, 'longer route' led me to think turning right would make the journey shorter but also less interesting. I hesitated just inside the glass doors, watching people on the other side hurrying toward a multitude of destinations. And then it was as though I reached out, pushed the doors open, turned right, and began to walk down the street. I say, 'as though' because I could see pedestrians on all sides of me, and I joined in the jostling crowd, happily making my way toward the corner where I planned to turn east, to venture through the midday chill.

Yet, in fact, I never moved. Never opened the doors at all. And when the desk clerk took hold of my elbow and asked, "Ma'am, would you like to sit down?" I let him guide me away from the lobby to an open area behind several enormous, velvet-leafed potted plants.

Tables had been set up for guests to enjoy meals from the hotel restaurant. I sat at one of these tables and the clerk placed a glass of water in front of me. Soon a waiter, slender and callow, flung open the metal French doors to the kitchen and conveyed to my table a meal I still don't recall ordering. A chicken sandwich with buttered bread, three sliced carrot sticks, and a pot of very hot, very strong, black tea.

With every bite of the sandwich I felt more keenly how ravenous my appetite had become. Only when I had cleaned my plate and swallowed the last drop of tea did I notice three middle aged women seated at the next table. They wore close-fitting hats which might have given them a vintage style if their dresses had not looked homemade and unfashionable, more like house dresses than outfits to wear while shopping for whatever was in the half dozen bags clustered around their feet. They were staring at me, one with her teacup poised midway to her lips.

A co-worker who had lived in London for a year offered me a list of social tips before I left home, to make my trip to the UK 'more pleasant.' Most of the rules were more offensive than helpful.

"Eat slowly, taking time to cut your meat into small bites. Tear bread into sections and butter each section, rather than slathering butter onto a whole slice and cramming it into your mouth. Don't say 'thank you' over and over. Say it once and then be quiet. Don't bring up politics under any circumstances but if you're confronted by questions about wars launched by your country, don't brag and do *not* claim any victory, moral or otherwise. Don't brush your teeth or floss in a public toilet. Never cut in line or demand special treatment.

"Above all, don't give the impression that you think

you're important. They hate that. In fact, they hate us, but they're much too polite to say so. Not like the French, who live to show their contempt for our disgusting habits and ignorance. No. British people simply stand back and wait for us to fall on our faces."

You would think we were born in a barn, if you listened to this woman talk. And there I was, finishing off my first meal since I'd arrived, and I'd somehow made a spectacle of myself. The women at the next table went on staring at me while I signed for the meal. I made my way out of the dining area toward the elevator. (No use calling it a 'lift,' the word doesn't describe that lurching sensation any better than the American term.)

I intended to freshen up, splash cold water on my face, and start out again. But the elevator ride, the cramped quarters combined with that too-swift, trundling motion, left me dispirited and sleepy. In the corridor I turned to the right and stopped. Somehow I'd lost my bearings. I must have taken a different route this time. The room numbers ascended toward the right, rather than descending. I turned left and soon found 309. In the privacy of my narrow room with its tousled sheets – I'd forgotten to leave the housekeeping sign on the door – I lay down and cried.

It occurs to me that I might be coming down with a cold. But the only symptoms are a weakened disposition and a craving for sleep.

~

Sept 26

I've been lying in bed staring out the window since 6 a.m. The sooty clouds threaten a malevolent downpour and I'd like to stay here re-reading Muriel Watson's biography. But I'll soon have to check into the next room I've reserved.

The ceiling over my bed is the one surface that doesn't appear to have been painted or repaired. I might be looking at the exact section of plaster Muriel saw, following her 'attempted coupling' with her mediocre poet. This is the phrase her biographer used to describe the grappling that occurred, not in this bed, it's too new, but in a bed exactly like it. After which Muriel awoke in this corner, with the gray, dim light from the window breaking across skewed sheets and sprawled bodies. How long did they lie here, reassembling their thoughts, wishing to be rid of one another?

In a month Davies would be gone, last seen stepping into the path of an oncoming laundry truck, an absurd death Muriel would immortalise in her second novel, *Gin and Tonic*. By then she'd given up hope of earning enough money from writing, and had returned to teaching. How she hated that. She hated children. She hated not being able to smoke when she wanted. A woman of her day, with a two-pack-a-day habit she picked up as a girl of twelve in this hotel, imitating the maids who cleaned the rooms, traipsing along when they climbed the fire escape to the roof for a midday smoke.

~

Sept 26

If she had won any of the awards (including a Booker Prize) for which her novels were nominated in 1969, 1973, and 1975, she might have been successful. She would belong to the world, and everyone would know her name. Even her biography is out of print, a hastily written profile by a long-dead author for hire. Published by The Arts Council in the late 1970s.

I found Muriel several years ago, in the farthest back corner of a musty book shop in Seattle, Washington. I'd lost my job, lost the apartment I shared with a younger, more successful technical editor named Giselle, who had informed me one day that she could, "no longer live with the stench of failure everywhere." She was nice enough to refund my deposit and first month's rent.

I moved across the street to an older building, into a basement studio. It was brutally cold in the winter and I made a habit of taking the bus once a day, to warm up. One of the regular stops was in the U-District, near Burton's Books. It was a rundown place, the only entrance via cobbled alley, its façade bearing a plaque attributing construction to a WPA crew.

Inside the shop, the air was a piquant mixture of patchouli and mildew. Books, many of them yellowed with age, crowded every surface and cluttered the aisles. Little towers of them leaned against chairs and shelves. Each aisle led to a quiet haven containing an armchair where patrons were welcome to sit and read as long as they liked. This became my world for the winter, and on into the cold, rainy spring, until I finally landed a new work assignment downtown.

In my favourite spot at Burton's Books a dilapidated crimson chair, decorated with crocheted doilies, faced a particularly dusty and neglected shelf. There a few Beryl Bainbridge novels met the tattered remnants of

Bloomsbury Group essays and biographies. And someone had placed Muriel Watson's novels on the end, out of any order I could imagine and far from the highbrow classics occupying the front of the shop. All three books appeared to be untouched, unread, as if the set were opened on a long ago Christmas morning and immediately discarded.

In my depression and weariness, I accepted this meeting as something like destiny. I opened the first volume, *The Glass Houses*, and began to read.

The first page described a hotel lobby, and a room very much like the one I occupy now. The narrator moved on to the streets, pubs, houses, and factories beyond the hotel, creating an atmosphere of undeniable gloom made bearable by the author's wit.

Alice was terribly pleased with herself. Nine o'clock. On any typical day she would be seated at her desk by now, surrounded by the awful rumble of morning gossip...

I felt an intangible and, given the geographic and chronological distance between us, inexplicable connection to Alice, and to Muriel. She was young, when she wrote this novel. She was engaged and fiercely determined to climb out of her own skin, and her hometown, using only words as a vehicle. Haven't we all had a dream like that?

I read that first novel in one sitting, at Burton's Books, and then bought all three. Online I tracked down a paperback of Muriel Watson's only biography. I traced her journey from the Hyde Hotel of her childhood, to the bedsit of her doomed poet in Islington, to a caravan on the beach where she spent a wild summer with friends who moved to Italy and never returned.

Muriel moved back here, to the street where she was born. After her parents died she lived on teaching wages and bravado, reading her work on the radio a few times, getting respectable reviews and award nominations, never quite able to escape the inertia of her time and place, never making crucial connections that could have led to festival readings and paid magazine writing. She joked in a radio interview that she was, "shaking off the dust and going on holiday."

Holidays she spent here, at the Hyde Hotel, trying to write. In this room, 219. The one to which I relocated at check-in.

There is no view, not even a crack of sky above the rooftops. The ceiling is stained a light amber from a past life, an era of evening cocktails and round-the-clock cigarettes. Hundreds of them smoked by Muriel as she sat staring at ominous white pages in her typewriter, her heart frozen to its purpose, fingers itching to do the only thing she knew how to do.

Did she realise she would only produce these three slender volumes of fiction? Her books were meant to be her escape. Yet who would read them? *An Unworthy Cause* would be her last novel. After a few decades, following her death, no one recalls her name. She isn't even listed in a recent *Guardian* round-up of the most obscure and forgotten British female authors.

Only I remember. Or seem to remember. Since she was dead by the time I learned of her life. Here are her books, on the nightstand, come home. I reach out and touch the brittle covers as I begin to drift off, bone tired after a day of disappointment.

~

Sept 27

Awakened in the middle of the night by the sound of someone trying to open my door. Pulling at the doorknob, rattling the key. I sat up in bed and turned on the light. But whoever was outside had moved on.

In the next moment I felt a wave of hunger that nearly knocked me over. Realising I had eaten only a sandwich in the past 24 hours, I picked up the phone to see if room service was operating, and discovered there was no tone at all. The phone didn't seem to be connected. So I wrapped myself in my robe, pulled on slippers, and, clutching the room key in my hand, crept out into the hall.

Every door in the corridor was open, though dimly lit, and on each doorstep people stood talking, their words indecipherably soft and low. I took a step and one of these conversational groups broke apart, a man in a brown suit touching the brim of his fedora as I passed. From another room a girl of seven or eight jumped across the threshold and darted ahead of me. I felt another wave of hunger and decided to go downstairs to the kitchen. Surely someone would be there, if not cooking, then preparing for the breakfast hour.

My legs were unsteady but I forced myself toward the elevator. When I heard the bell indicating the door was open, I found the girl was already aboard. I followed. She didn't look at me, didn't speak, and I decided not to make conversation. There are parents who encourage their children to be sociable with adults, and many more who don't. I chose to err on the side of caution in case the girl's mother had a rule about not talking to strangers.

The elevator ride made me dizzy. I had to take a deep breath when we landed. The second the doors parted and the girl stepped out, the tantalising aroma of bacon and eggs reached me. I let my hunger lead me down a passage with streaky black stains, apparent scars from years of food trolleys banging against the walls. The floor was slightly raked toward a set of metal doors, propped open, with bright light spilling out.

Among the steam tables, knives, pots and pans, a heavyset woman wearing a hairnet and white apron stood talking to the girl from the elevator. The woman held up one hand and seemed to be lecturing the child, who twitched and shrugged under her steady gaze. When I stepped into the doorway, both looked at me and froze. I heard a thousand minute voices murmuring. The hotel coming to life just before dawn, waking and stretching, putting a kettle on, dropping bread into a toaster, pulling on a clean shirt, lathering soap in a shaving cup, washing hands and face, sweeping the front doorstep, placing a sign on the pavement, opening curtains and blinds...

I woke up in my bed a few minutes ago. On the nightstand next to my books I found a small tray with toast and eggs, bacon, fried tomato, and a pot of tea. My head aches. I drink the tea in gulps, with generous helpings of sugar, and I eat with gusto, since no one can see me and take offence.

~

Sept 28

Nothing to report other than rest and reading. I fell asleep again yesterday, right after breakfast, and slept all day.

My itinerary is ruined. I no longer expect to visit Muriel's favourite bookshop, or the school where she taught grammar and composition to the children she called, "an unworthy cause." It's all I can do to lie here, propped up by stiff, uncooperative pillows, re-reading her books.

There is an arc to her fiction. Beginning with the youthful jaunt, the green, lively attitude of *The Glass Houses*. The first chapter was written years before the rest, when the author was in school. It serves as a time capsule, then, an indication of her expectations.

"I will leave all of this, someday," the protagonist tells her mother. Yet by the final chapter the outcome is less certain, and we're left wondering if the bright, opinionated young woman will strike out on her own or spend her life working as a secretary at an insurance firm.

Gin and Tonic is more measured in tone. Its central characters make no pronouncements about the future. The only humour arises from the contrast between the protagonist's view of herself and the things others say about her. She rails against her fate as her mother's caretaker and part-time clerk at a company so boring she fails to identify its purpose. But she doesn't make plans to run away.

The old lady had taken a tumble. So said the pockmarked social worker from Hackney, who wore too much lipstick and badly scuffed high heels. The calmness of her voice assured everyone that a common accident had occurred, and there was no need for alarm.

Most of Muriel's third novel was written in this penultimate room. Afterward she struggled but failed to find a new story. Darker and more mature than her first two books, *An Unworthy Cause* alternates between an elementary school and a nursing home where the endless routine of meals, deadly entertainments, and bedpan collection add up to existential resignation. Life is sorrow and the sooner we accept it the better, the author seems to say. The few overtly comic moments are cruel in their depiction of elderly dementia and physical decay.

In a little while I'll be changing rooms again. This will require more energy than I have at the moment. So I'll rest now, and try to rally in time.

~

Sept 29

Room 206 is both more comfortable and more sterile than my previous accommodations. I wonder if Muriel chose it for these reasons. She knew the hotel better than anyone. She must have wanted a quiet corner in which to spend her last day. Or am I imagining? Nothing in her biography indicates that she planned, in advance, to end her life when she checked into the Hyde Hotel for a final visit. I've drawn my conclusion from the fact that she stayed in this room and not her usual 219, the one in which she wrote her books, and later on tried to write, so painfully and unsuccessfully.

In these misted, green hills, are the premature buds wasting away, lured to their destiny by a brief, false Spring?

The ending line to her last novel. Without words, Muriel had no life. She must have come to this room with a purpose. I believe that. After all, what is a writer without words?

I'm scheduled to begin the long journey back home tomorrow. To my basement studio. To rain and silence, to long hours downtown, surrounded by young people who find my sweaters too bulky, my hair too gray, my inability to discern their jokes amusing, my questions (as I work my way through their appalling documents) a sign of mental sluggishness. I don't watch the shows they watch, or listen to their music, or appreciate the nuances of their code.

Trying not to think of all that I've missed on this trip. If I think of it, I'll fall. Down that long, blinding chasm. My failure to trace Muriel's steps, to see what she saw, to know better than anyone alive what it must have been to create the world inside her books, this weighs on me and I can barely record the details. But one odd thing has occurred and I'm compelled to mention it.

I must have fallen asleep with one hand under my head. When I woke up I was groggy and sick. I fumbled my way to the bathroom, an obviously added feature so confining I bang my elbows on the sink and shower stall if I'm not careful. In the stark light I could see, clearly imprinted across my face, the bright pink ovals of three fingerprints.

I've been drinking water, glass after glass, but I'm still too tired to go outside in the corridor. The phone buzzes when I pick it up; when I dial, nothing happens.

If I just wait here, quietly, keeping my energy in reserve, I'm sure the desk clerk will send a porter eventually. When check-out time arrives and I fail to appear. When the maids lose patience and unlock the door, to get on with their rounds. When someone comes. When something happens.

HH Lost & Found Inventory Item, handwritten journal, cover partially torn. No identification.

S P Miskowski

Housekeeping

I have killed myself, the note said.

Debbie glanced up and down the corridor. It was empty.

I have killed myself.

The note had been left on the floor, emerging from beneath the door as if pushed from the other side, though someone must have come out to hook the 'PLEASE CLEAN MY ROOM' card over the handle. The note was a single sheet of white A4 folded in half. *For the cleaner,* it said on the facing side. Debbie had been struck by the neat handwriting and the purple ink. Who wrote in purple? She'd picked up the note carefully, hoping for a tip inside. She only found more writing.

> *Do not come in. I have killed myself. I apologise that it had to be here. Please notify your manager – you should not have to deal with this.*

Debbie swiped her master key through the lock slot and nudged the door open with her behind, pulling the cleaning cart in behind her. She glanced into the bedroom.

Nobody there.

No body.

Instead of propping the door open with the cleaning cart like she usually did, Debbie brought it all the way inside and let the door close behind her.

The bedroom was tidy. The bed was made, covers tight across the mattress and turned down at one corner exactly as was standard practice. It hadn't been slept in. The teas and coffees hadn't been touched, the cups and drinking glasses still upside down on their tray. The television remote was beside them on top of the hotel information sheet. Next to that, a set of car keys, the hotel room card, and a fountain pen. Purple ink, Debbie presumed. A man's suit jacket was draped over the chair, something good but old, buttons hanging loose on their threads. A pair of shoes pointed their toes under the dressing table, a sock stuffed into each one.

Debbie looked to the door leading to the bathroom. It was closed.

Do not come in.

She went to the door – "Hello?" – and turned her ear towards it. Nothing. She knocked. "Hello? Housekeeping. Are you okay?"

I have killed myself...

Debbie opened the door.

A man lay in the shower cubicle.

I apologise that it had to be here.

The shower curtain had been bunched up and cast over the rail, just like Debbie did when she cleaned inside. The man was slumped in the corner, mostly upright and almost sitting, held up by a cord he'd tied around his neck to the shower controls.

I have killed myself...

A clear plastic bag over his head had been sucked close to his face, his mouth open in a dark O behind it. The cord around his neck held the bag in place.

I have killed myself...

He had slit his wrists, too. Blood had pooled in the dimples of the non-slip matt beneath him and faint splashes on the tiled walls suggested the shower had been running for some of the time the man bled away down the drain.

I have killed myself.

Yeah, Debbie thought. You really have. Though it wasn't like she hadn't been warned. Her tip: do not come in.

She lowered the toilet seat and sat down, staring into the shower cubicle.

The man was barefoot but otherwise still dressed, trousers soaked and bloody, shirt sleeves rolled. Debbie wondered if it was to avoid the embarrassment of post mortem nudity or if he'd done it as a consideration for those who would find him. There was a smear of blood across the temperature dial where he'd managed to turn the power off to save water. She wondered how long he'd waited before doing so, sucking final strangled breaths out of the plastic bag. One of his hands was reaching to the drain; a tidy bleed-out. The wrist was open wider than she thought was needed, and it seemed more black than red, a dark gaping grin above his palm. Debbie couldn't look away, except to look at the contortions of his face. Wrist. Face. No grin on his face. His mouth was open, the rest of his features blurred behind plastic wet with condensation.

When Debbie was able to turn away she saw herself in the mirror above the sink. She was as pale as the tiles around her.

There was another note.

Several sheets of A4 this time, folded in half again but standing in the gap behind the taps like a paper tent.

Dearest...

Debbie reached for it. The paper had wrinkled slightly in the moisture of the room but the ink had not run.

Dearest...

She held it in her lap a moment then unfolded it.

The man had filled each page and he wrote small, thin lines of neat purple script. He'd signed it. There was a name to go with his face. With his wrists.

Debbie didn't know him. Not yet.

She read the note.

What she read did not match the considerate man she'd imagined, and probably didn't match what others thought of him either, judging by his anxious apologies. At one confession Debbie gasped and dropped the papers, retrieving them quickly because parts of the floor were still wet. She shuffled them together and folded them in her lap. She glanced at the man leaning in the shower, opened the pages again and continued reading.

She swore. She cried. She read it again, this purple prose goodbye. Eventually she stood. She folded the note and held it.

"Bastard."

He said only 'oh', though when she left he implored her to stay, reaching for her with a limp smiling hand.

Debbie pushed her cleaning trolley out into the corridor. She shut the door.

She left the trolley outside the room and headed for the front desk. As she waited for the elevator, another note hushed into the corridor from under one of the opposite doors.

Sometimes it happened this way. She'd been warned it would be... *strange*, working here. Sometimes difficult. She was only recently realising the extent of that.

She wasn't permitted to interfere.

Please notify your manager...

The other note, *Dearest*, she placed in the pocket of her apron. She would keep it. She didn't know who *Dearest* was—

...you should not have to deal with this...

—but she thought it was better not to know.

Ray Cluley

Something Like Blood

The red pen scratches halfway across the page before it gives up, leaving a crimson blotch as its death throe. The patch glistens wetly.

"Oh, I am sorry about that, Mr Holden. I'll just fetch another."

The old man behind the counter dodders away, pushing into what must be a back office. Michael shakes the pen, trying to extort a little more life from it, but there's nothing else to be done. The receptionist returns a moment later, empty-handed.

"I'm sorry about that, Mr Holden. I suppose half a signature will have to do. Would you like me to show you to your room?"

"No, no. That won't be necessary."

"It's room 109, first floor, left at the top of the stairs."

"Thank you."

Michael grabs the handle of his bag and wheels it behind him as he makes his way to his room.

The deep red walls and the black carpet of the Hyde don't exactly provide the warmest of welcomes.

~

The door to Room 109 swings open, and Michael pushes his bag in ahead of him. Nothing too bad – a single bed, clean white, stark against the continually black carpet. The wallpaper is patterned, faded from red to pink. Good enough, for the time being. He sits down with a thump on the bed, which slumps softly beneath him. It feels warm, too, which surprises him. Probably only just been cleaned and dried.

The Hyde Hotel. The name brings him a chuckle – what better place *to* hide? Innocuous, old-fashioned, nondescript, far enough from home that no-one should think to look for him here, but not so far to suggest he's running from anything. No use crashing anywhere fancy, or roughing it in a hostel – no, this'll do nicely. Hidden in plain sight.

It's not a long-term answer, of course, but a decent enough temporary one.

He unpacks what he hopes is a week's worth of clothing – newly bought from town, nothing like his usual fare. All his shirts, ties and jackets remain at the house – an expensive remainder of his old life. But why not take this moment to break from tradition? T-shirts with garish logos, short trousers, hoodies. The door to the cupboard reveals that it has no back, just the pink patterned wall showing behind it. Shrugging, he hangs eight sets of clothing on the rail and proceeds to dress for dinner.

~

One week's stay, paid up-front, with meals. Perhaps going for meals was something of a risk, not knowing exactly how it would be, but he wanted to make sure there was no reason to go anywhere else. Sure, most likely no-one would be looking for him, but why take the chance? The Hyde will be his home for seven days – perhaps even more, depending on the coming week. He descends the stairs, marvelling at the freedom offered by the loose-fitting t-shirt and unbelted trousers. He's been so long in a suit the feeling is practically revelatory.

He reaches the lobby again, and a brief scan of the area doesn't reveal the restaurant. He heads to the reception, the same elderly man waiting for him. "Good evening, Mr Holden."

"Evening. I've just come down for dinner, but I can't seem to find the restaurant?"

"Oh yes." He takes a long sniff before continuing. "It's downstairs. I'm afraid the lift's out of order, so you'll have to take the stairs."

"No problem."

There's nothing to indicate the lift is out of order, but Michael descends the steps anyway and finds himself immediately walking into a spacious restaurant. It's far too big for the scale of the hotel, in all honesty. The room hums with a sort of fallen grandeur, a chandelier with a few broken strands of glass, an elegant wallpaper much at odds with the rest of the building. A young waiter, a little hunched, heads to welcome him. Without a word he indicates the direction to Michael's table. He doesn't even ask for a room number, and Michael isn't inclined to give it. The uneasy gait and curious eye of the greeter unsettles him, and he's pleased when a beaming girl, probably no more than eighteen, comes over to take his drink order. A few moments later his pint of lager arrives, cast a ruddy shade in the light of the chandelier. He takes a deep draught, and reflects that his drink looks something like…

"What can I get you for dinner, sir?" The waitress asks as she appears beside him. He catches a shard of her perfume, flowery and pleasant.

"Oh, I'm sorry, I haven't even looked." He grabs the menu awkwardly, fumbling like a nervous teenager before finally getting it open. He's very conscious of her leaning over him, the proximity of her aromatic skin, and makes a snap decision on dinner: steak, medium to well done.

"No problem at all. Thank you." With a broad grin she takes the menu away and trots artlessly back to the kitchen. Michael is conscious that he's alone in the restaurant. He's also conscious that he likes the feeling. No pressure, no one looking at him, judging him. He could eat the steak with his hands for all it mattered. He takes another draw from his pint, and wonders about ordering another. He can feel it helping him unwind already.

The steak arrives, and the waitress clumps it down in front of him. A splash of béarnaise sauce lands on her hand as she does so. "Oh no," she whispers, before proceeding to lick it away. She looks at Michael intently as she does this, and Michael can feel an erection rising despite himself. "Enjoy," she says as she strolls away. Michael tries to shake off a slightly dirty feeling. Picking up his knife and fork, he cuts into the meat deeply, and a gush of blood spews forth. He sighs. *Rare.* Not in the least how he asked for it. There's no-one in the restaurant to speak to about it, so he pops a few of the vegetables in his mouth. The taste of the spreading blood still lingers in it, so he spits out his mouthful tactlessly. He waits for another minute or two, wondering if anyone else will emerge to serve him, but after that he gives up and heads back upstairs.

~

Back in his bedroom, he kicks off his shoes and undresses. A reflex draws him towards the shower, but he pauses as his hand touches the bathroom doorknob. No need. No need at all. He stands there, naked, just for a moment. No need to bath, or shower, or shave. He simply climbs into bed – his still warm and cosy bed. As he lays there, his mind filling with all the events on the day, he thinks once again of his waitress and the length of her tongue, the shape of her arse as she walked away, and does something else that once would have been off limits to him.

~

Morning rolls around, and Michael clambers from the bed and opens the window. The view offers nothing at all – far-off industrial estates and dilapidated car parks. It has its own broken, urban, lifeless appeal. No one to see his nudity, and who cares if they did? He's got nothing much to be ashamed of, he reflects. Again the impulse to shower rises in him, and again he fights his programming. He carelessly throws on some clothes and heads down for breakfast. At the lobby, he is greeted once again by the ageing receptionist, still standing in the same place as he was last night. Michael has an impression of him never moving, a sentinel watching over his crumbling dominion. On the way downstairs he sees the same waitress from last night, and she brushes close past him on the way up. Did she need to brush that close? She says nothing, but Michael wonders if she can sense his shame in some way. The closeness of her body brings back those same feelings, and he hopes that she isn't serving for breakfast.

She isn't, and after a functional meal, Michael returns to his room, wondering what to do with his day. He didn't bring much with him – after all, he packed in a fair hurry. There's always the option of TV, but a flick through the daytime offerings offers slim pickings. Remarkably, there are only five channels, practically ancient technology by today's standards. He didn't bring a book, or his laptop – nothing at all. Perhaps that's for the best in a way – leave it all behind, with the clothes and the expensive stereo and her. He decides to head down to the bar, sit with a newspaper for a while, perhaps even see if he can strike up any conversation.

~

A couple of hours later, he returns to his room, frustrated. The bar at the Hyde was just as deserted as the restaurant – Michael wonders to himself if there are even other guests staying. With a couple of dailies read, there was nothing else to be done, short of getting on the booze early. With few other options, he lays in bed for a while.

The knock on the door gives him a start – he must have dropped off again. Why not? No one to please but himself, no demands, no deadlines. He climbs off the bed

– warm with the heat of his body – swiftly dresses and opens the door.

"Sorry to disturb you, sir. I've come to clean the room."

Michael doesn't reply for a moment. He looks her up and down, and she gives no sign of recognising him at all. It's the waitress from last night, in another role as the cleaner. Even her scent is the same.

"Of course. Sorry, I must have dozed off."

"No problem."

"They keep you busy here, huh?" he says.

"I'm sorry, sir?"

"Well, you were working last night, and at breakfast."

"I've only just arrived, sir. You must have me confused with someone else."

"Yes, of course."

Of course, he tells himself. Of course. She squeezes past him with that quirky smile. Of course it can't be her.

But it is. *It is.* Down to the finest detail, even that awkward but somehow sexy stride as she moves.

He watches her open the door to the bathroom, debating whether to stay in the room or head back to the bar. For the moment he is transfixed with simply watching her. "Are you all right, sir?" she asks innocently.

"Yes, sorry. Of course."

"It's just... well... there's some blood in the sink. You haven't... hurt yourself?"

"Hurt? No. Blood?" He steps to the bathroom, and she's right – around the plughole of the sink is a distinctive splash of red.

"I... I haven't been in the bathroom since I checked in. This must be from whoever stayed here last."

"Are you all right, sir?" She reaches out and grabs his arm; the contact sends a static shock through him.

"I think so. I wasn't expecting..."

"Of course not. Just leave it to me, sir. If you come back in an hour, I'll be all done." She smiles, warmly, an expression he hasn't seen from her before.

"Yes. Thank you." Michael drifts out, another trip to the bar awaiting him.

~

Michael sits uneasily, this time having given in to the temptation for a pint. It's not sitting right, and taking him a long time to get down. It's so thick in his throat he gives up at halfway. The barman seems to have vanished, so he can't even order anything else. He can only sit with his head resting on the table for a while, before a gentle hand on his shoulder prompts him to look up. "Your room is all ready, sir. I'm so sorry about that. I'll make sure management know about it."

"Thank you. I appreciate it."

"I have to ask again, sir... are you all right? You look... unhappy."

Michael smiles wryly. "I suppose I am."

"Would you like me to do anything?"

He wants to say, *would you hold me*, but the words sound utterly ridiculous in his mind. How long since a woman – or anyone – held him?

"No, I'll be OK. Thank you." She squeezes his shoulder gently before walking away. Her softness almost breaks him, and he barely makes it to his bedroom before the tears arrive.

~

He checks himself in the bathroom before heading down to dinner. He hasn't showered – still exercising that element of control – but he wants to make sure he looks the best he possibly can besides that. The waitress – the maid? – is still on his mind, and he wants to look presentable. It's a strange feeling – all his preening was usually driven by...

Go on, say it.

"Sylvia." The word surprises him by coming out of his lips rather than staying in his subconscious.

Sylvia, Sylvia. Beautiful, cruel, *in the past* Sylvia. Sylvia he left behind, with his possessions and his existence. He refuses to call it a life.

But now there are new chances, new possibilities. With a final flick of his hair, he leaves his room.

~

The restaurant does a far better job of his second evening's dining – he was scarcely filled with confidence after yesterday, but the roast chicken and fudge cake are surprisingly palatable. The Hyde doesn't serve haute cuisine, but he's had plenty of that for the time being. But what makes the evening even more enjoyable is the fact that his favourite waitress is on duty again. He is still unable to distinguish her from the cleaner. Perhaps the two are twins? That must be it, he tells himself. It can only be that. They might even be playing something of a game with him, and that thought excites him all the more. Because the game can only have one end, surely? He hasn't played that game for a long time, mind.

"Is that everything you wanted, sir?" she pops up at this side, interrupting something between daydream and sexual fantasy. The smile she wears gives the question a hint of innuendo. "That's all for food, thanks."

"Good. And how was everything?"

"Delicious. Great."

"Can I get you a coffee, anything else to drink?"

"No, thank you. Can I ask you a question?"

"Of course."

"Do you have a sister?"

"A sister? No, I'm an only child. Why do you ask?"

"Nothing, nothing. Look, can I ask you something else?"

"Of course."

And he asks a question he hasn't asked anybody since her. Since Sylvia.

~

The evening passes in a haze, but Michael doesn't mind. So much of the world around him feels vague, but in contrast he sees *her* with an absolute clarity. She's in sharp focus; nothing around her matters. He watches her eyes, the seductive glint there, the shape of her body as she slouches in her seat, a relaxed sexuality he's never seen before. He listens to her voice, and it seems as though each word carries some additional meaning, a philosopher with the voice of a butterfly's wings. Could he love her? Perhaps he could love her. But he has to do something first. He has to *have* her. With each drop of alcohol, each moment he spends in her company, each dripping-with-definition sentence, the thought lodges and refuses to let go.

He never asks her name, because what he feels transcends that. Did he ask her to come to his room, or was it her idea? He can't even recall. Maybe they never even spoke it, but communicated it with something deeper. They kiss by his door, lips melding, folding into one another, a tactility he has never experienced before. The door opens – was the key involved in that?–and they tumble into the room, the carpet catching them with fibres like blades of black grass.

He strips – or does she strip him? – and his senses are heightened further as his flesh is exposed to the air, to the little worms of her fingers and the fat caterpillar of her tongue. He can feel his erection throbbing, a thick centipede, her fingers brushing against the fleshy carapace. With a deep breath, he moves to mouth her name, but realises he doesn't know it.

She moves her mandibles away from him, pushing him even deeper into the carpet beneath him. The black transforms into red, red, *crimson*, as the blades of grass cut at him, a delicious pain writhing through his body

Her form looms over him, and he cannot wait to taste her, to dig deep into the earth and soil that makes her. And it tastes something like...

Something like copper. Something like...

Something like *perfection*. He drinks of her, and he feels as though his whole world is turning to liquid, and he is drowning, and he doesn't care whether he breathes or not...

~

He wakes up in the morning, alone, in bed. Michael doesn't remember moving there, but they must have done at some point. The previous night feels fragmentary, but each memory is lucidly clear, a reflective shard of pleasure among so many.

He lays for a while, moving, turning only occasionally. But each time he moves, he swears he can feel wetness beneath him. It could be any number of things, and it's only when he concedes to pull the sheet back and allow the day to begin that he can see what it is.

Blood. *Her* blood?

It doesn't matter. He curls himself up again, deciding that he might as well make the most of the last of her warmth. The sheet is comforting around him, and he decides that today there's no need to go anywhere. He came to the Hyde Hotel to lay low, and that's exactly his intention.

~

There's a knock on the door some time later. The time could be anything. He doesn't even want to answer it, so he decides not to. A moment later he hears a click and the door swings open. For just a second he thinks it's her, but as his vision solidifies he sees that it's the cleaner again. She moves into the room and sets about her tasks wordlessly, without disturbing him. The white noise of the Hoover almost puts him to sleep, and the next thing he knows she is leaning over him in bed, pulling the sheets back. Oh god, that essence of perfume again...

"My my, you have gotten in a mess," she says, pushing his body to one side and starting to scrub furiously at the stains left on the bed.

But they won't come clean. Why won't they come clean?

Then he sees it. The brush is making the red stains even worse, not making them better. And the bucket she dips it into is the same shade of red...

She hums, and the sound is soothing. It all seems fine. It all seems *right*. But there's one thing he needs to know.

"Who are you?"

"Me? You don't know?"

"I feel like... maybe..."

"Sylvia. It's Sylvia."

And she continues to scrub away at the bed, growing more and more crimson with each passing moment. Maybe it's the colour it's supposed to be, Michael thinks to himself. But all he wants is for her to leave, to leave so he can go back to sleep. But with the gentle sound of the caustic brushing on the bed, he finds himself drifting, drifting...

Sylvia...

~

The next time he wakes up he's conscious of the moisture beneath him. For a groggy moment he wonders if he is swimming, but as he turns to the shape beside him, he is reassured by the spring of the mattress beneath him. "Hi, honey," he mumbles. He doesn't know who it is laid next to him. The voice that speaks next to him is snail-trail smooth, soft and sickening. "Good morning, honey. I was starting to think you'd never wake up."

"I'm just tired, Sylvia."

"Tired. Of course." The voice starts sweet, but soon turns cloying. "You've been working so many late nights."

"Nights? Nights? I haven't... I don't... I'm off work, you know that."

"Off? You need some time off, but you're so dedicated, Michael. You do work hard."

"I just... I want the best for us. For you."

"I know. But you can't give it to me, can you? You try and you try, but it leaves me wondering..."

"Wondering what, honey?"

"Wondering what life would have been like with somebody like..."

Somebody like... like...

There are more words, but it doesn't matter. His hands are on her throat now, and he squeezes, squeezes, feeling the flesh give way beneath his hands like dough, like paper mache, like a cushion stitched from skin...

And as his nails dig in, like ten infinitesimal blades, monomolecular...

And he can feel the first drops of...

Something like...

~

The room feels oppressive when he awakens. The heat radiates from everywhere, as well as a rank odour that makes him feel like complaining to the desk. How can they let someone sleep in this room? It's... inhumane. *Inhuman.*

As the light of dawn cracks through the curtains, he can see the source of the swelter in the room. The walls, the floor, even the ceiling are painted a hideous shade of crimson. Something like...

Something like blood.

No, not *like* blood.

Michael makes an effort to rise from bed, to move, but

it simply feels like too much hard work in the choking air and the attacking heat. He lays down, down, in the aqueous redness of his bed, and begins to sink... and sink... and sink...

And soon enough the smell of metal is not frightening, but comforting, like perfume...

~

The old man stands at the door, looking into room 109. After those strange reports from both one of the waitresses and one of the maids – he thinks one of them is called Sylvia, but he doesn't have the head for names that he used to – he had to look into it.

As he surveys the scene, he knows that another one has gone. In the bed, the man staying there – what was his name? – is constricted in the sheets, a mummy entombed in cotton. He pulls the material away from the head, just to confirm what he already knows.

He knows the look, like he's known the look on so many before. *Guilt*. No doubt about it – the Hyde brings these things out of people. That and other things.

He wonders whether this time he should call the police or simply leave it to the cleaning staff. As he leaves the room, he catches a faint smell in the air.

Something like...

Alex Davis

The Coyote Corporation's Misplaced Song

Arthur Charles Manfred Edwards, resting against the hotel room door, handle poking into his back and fire emergency poster affixing itself to his bald patch, clutched the bomb to his chest. The bomb, which for the purposes of the story we'll name Lullaby, was a traditional cartoon version of a bomb, a little airship-like in shape and gold in colour. Arthur didn't know much about bombs, only slightly more than Lullaby who thought itself a six-year-old boy. Children scared Arthur.

When a school for complicated children opened across the street from his bungalow, Arthur had retreated into the larder and stayed there until the stink in his trousers knocked out a visiting rat and he'd run out of bourbon biscuits. He'd shaken off another rat, which made a meal of his shoelaces, and opened the larder door. The sounds of the schoolchildren were louder, but Arthur surmised that would be because there was now a hole in his bungalow roof, letting in outside annoyances. He hadn't suspected the sounds emanated from the unexploded bomb that sat on his favourite chair surrounded by shattered roof slates and showered with plaster dust.

Back in the hotel room, Arthur's heart ticked louder than the bomb, which didn't tick in the usual sense. There was certainly nothing clockwork or digital about it. Lullaby offered more of a hiccup. Arthur turned to look through the spy hole; the emergency poster flapping from his head replaced the 'kick here' note of childhood. The hallway looked empty, but children were short and he wouldn't necessarily see them at this height. He caught no shadows.

Arthur dropped onto the bed, still clutching the bomb. Despite the location of his room (fifth floor) and the closed window, Arthur heard an ice cream van. Everyone knows children chase after ice cream vans in their hundreds.

Arthur Charles Manfred Edwards was prone to exaggeration, which, in his formative years, had proved a factor for adults not believing him when he'd *claimed* that his *friends* had made him sit in the centre of a circle while they clasped their hands and danced around him chanting dreadful things that made him feel smaller than a pea.

A discordant version of *Greensleeves* filled the room, rebounding off the tarnished mirror and the peeling wallpaper. It sounded as if the ice cream van was about to drive into his hotel room and take lodging in his brain.

"You're going mad old man," he said to his dishevelled image in the hotel mirror.

His trousers were pee-stained, his shirt sweat-stained. Arthur ripped the poster from his head, tearing free precious strands along with their follicles. What seemed like hours later, but was in fact seven minutes and twelve seconds, the hotel phone rang. Arthur ignored it the first three times. With each subsequent call, the bomb's hiccups increased. Although appearing calm, Lullaby bordered on tantrum, but Arthur couldn't know that. Arthur thought the bomb a bomb, and didn't understand the complex emotions attached. With great destructive power comes great responsibility. In truth, Lullaby only had enough fire power to take out Arthur, the room, and some of the corridor.

"Hello," Arthur said.

A moment of static, then a child's singsong voice said, "We'd like to speak to your companion." A pause, then the voice became gruffer, more adult. "Now."

"I have no companion," Arthur said, putting down the receiver.

Arthur's comment offended Lullaby so much he almost threw a tantrum. Of course, throwing a tantrum when you're a bomb and not a six-year-old boy is dangerous and liable to remove a gentleman's worries about bald spots, paunches and bad breath.

The phone rang again. Lullaby rocked on Arthur's knee. He wanted to answer the phone and declare himself kidnapped. Although, they were yet to decide who had kidnapped whom. This time, the ringing didn't stop. It wouldn't until Arthur answered. Its persistent call skipped from a familiar ring into a harpsichord version of Ring-a-Roses. Arthur fell down.

Lullaby rolled across the pattened carpet towards the door; bumping into the bedside table mid route. His insides rattled.

Digging fingernails into the fading carpet, Arthur

dragged himself up, grabbing hold of and knocking the phone off the bedside table in the process. His heart almost drowned out the voice that hissed from it.

"Hello," said a voice that was loud, clear and demanding. "Hello, hello, hello."

"Go away," Arthur said, refusing to touch the phone.

A hiss from the phone as if the caller or the technology considered the request.

"May I crawl out now?" the voice asked, followed by a childish giggle.

Again, Arthur tore at his already sparse hair. How had they followed him here? *Children, children everywhere and no net to catch them in.* When Arthur was a boy, the local bin men used to sing that to keep the local kids from climbing on the back of the lorry. *To stop the truck eating them*, his mother had claimed. It wasn't the truck that scared Arthur. It was the friends who put him in a metal bin and left him out for the bin men to collect. For reasons he'd never understood, he was the one that got the hiding that day.

He didn't want to catch any children. Goosebumps raised on Arthur's arms. If the world were under his command, he'd make all children run in the opposite direction to wherever he headed. If only he had knives for fingers and razors for teeth, snakes for hair and pincers for feet. They'd not bother him then. Arthur picked up the bomb and shook it. A hiccup sounded in place of a tick.

"May I?" asked the voice on the phone.

"You may not," Arthur said. "You may not. Go away. Shoo or the Bogey Man will get you."

A giggle replaced the voice. Arthur dared to grab the handset. He dropped it onto the phone, fingers slipping as he feared small fingers would reach out and grab his hand. With the call cut off, the phone began ringing again.

It rang. It rang. It rang. It rang. It rang. It rang.

Arthur switched on the television to drown out the incessant noise. After Arthur had flicked through seven channels, he and Lullaby settled back to watch a documentary about sharks that featured no children at all. In its turn, the sharks gave way to a documentary about the Second World War. Arthur patted Lullaby's back and said, "One for you." This confused Lullaby, who'd rather watch The Lone Ranger.

The phone rang and rang and rang.

Someone knocked at the door. Arthur muted the television. He looked at Lullaby (who believed he looked back). Arthur threw the thin duvet over Lullaby, and then climbed off the bed. The phone continued to ring. The hammer of his heart against his chest promised to drown out the call. Another knock.

"Who is it?" Arthur asked. He spat on his fingers, running them through his hair to bring some calm to the disarray.

"Bomb squad," the visitor said. "Ha! Ha! Only room service, sir."

Arthur's fingers twitched over his trouser pocket, where the room key rested.

"I didn't order..." Arthur began to say.

The man interrupted. "Compliments of the establishment, sir. Something to make your visit go with a bang, ha! Bangers and mash that is. Two servings on our finest crockery."

"There's only one of me."

Arthur looked about the room, frightened a child had slipped in behind him.

"The girl on the phone said there were two. If you could open the door, sir. The tray is heavy and if we leave the food any longer it'll need to be buried."

"Then bury it," Arthur said, although he was peckish. "I mean. How tall are you?"

For some reason, unknown even to him, Arthur stood on his tiptoes as if to appear taller. The phone rang louder.

"About six-four in my stocking feet and owner of the nickname, Lurch."

That was far too tall to be a child. On the bed, Lullaby tried to throw off the duvet but found it impossible to as he was a bomb and not a six-year-old boy. Lullaby began to cry, which came out more of a whine that threatened to take out a delightful bedside lamp with yellow tassels. Lullaby began to suspect he wasn't a boy of any age.

Sliding the card in the key card slot, Arthur opened the door. A long shadow crossed the threshold, stretching all the way to the window and possibly into the building across the street. Lurch ducked to enter the room and remained stooped throughout his visit.

"Is everything to your satisfaction?" Lurch asked, glancing at the phone. "There have been a number of complaints online about spiders, but spiders are everywhere and at least ours apologise for dangling down your ear hole. All our unexpected visitors introduce themselves."

Lurch placed the tray on the bedside table beside the vibrating phone. He picked up said phone, snapping its cord so the ringing ceased.

"There. We can't have unwanted persons crawling into your room, sir. Enjoy your meal and if you need anything else please call," Lurch said.

Lurch left, taking the telephone with him. Despite its absence, Arthur could still hear its ring, a tinnitus playing in his eardrums. He sat on the edge of the bed and ran a fork through the mash, which proved more gloop.

The television programme had changed from the war documentary to a breaking news flash about Arthur and Lullaby. There Arthur was walking along the street, clutching the bomb to his chest, while people ran away from him. He sort of remembered the screams, but thought they ran from the children who followed him. He saw those children now, on the television screen. Faces he recognised. William 'The Terror' Craven from his fifth year at school, and Mabel 'The Snake' Anderson from his nursery class, and worst of all, Albert 'Caveman' Marcelo from swimming who had held his head under the water and peed in his face.

Pacing from one side of the room to the other, Arthur found himself at the window. His fingers twitched at the net curtain. Police surrounded the hotel. Along the road, spectators played ghouls as they amassed behind yellow tape. The three children – William, Mabel and Albert – danced around the police officers, and at the point of Mabel's finger, all three looked up to his hotel room, to Arthur. They skipped towards the hotel. Arthur's fingers pressed against cold glass. He wanted to knock at the window, to lift the sash and scream at the police to stop his tormentors, but the lead policeman held a large gun, aiming it in the direction of Arthur's room. Arthur stepped back. Despite a collection of liver spots on cheeks and neck, Arthur was fond of his head. His knees gave way beneath him. Mid-fall, his nose kissed the windowsill and blood dripped onto his shirt.

A metallic-voice erupted from a megaphone on the street below. "Surrender."

"Leave me alone, leave me alone, leave me alone." Arthur tore at what little hair remained.

On the television, the newscaster told viewers that the suspected bomber had torn the phone from its socket; a hotel employee had told police that the suspect pitched it at the wall. The police urged people to stay away from there area, but assured there was no need for citizens to be alarmed.

Pressing the end of his shirt to his nose, Arthur wished he'd left the bomb on his favourite chair. He'd hoped its presence would scare away the children, but these kids thought themselves immortal. He'd cast them in their age of tormenting and moulded them there. A peek out the window offered a horrifying view. The three scurried up the sides of the hotel by way of the drainpipe. His fingers fumbled with the window lock, checking it was secure.

"They'll set off the bomb," Arthur said, with a whine.

The word 'bomb' frightened Lullaby. It threatened to take away his personality. His skin felt hot with fever, his insides swelled. If only he could throw off the duvet. Man and bomb burned. Arthur unbuttoned his shirt and fanned himself with the emergency poster.

A face at the window merged into William, Mabel and Albert's faces – a distortion of his greatest fears pounding at the glass, demanding entry. Arthur crawled onto the bed, knocking Lullaby off it in the process. Lullaby wanted to ask if he was a six-year-old boy or even a boy of any age, but he already suspected the answer. As Arthur Charles Manfred Edwards hated children, he would not take a child as his companion. Lullaby rattled his insides, aware of the parts that would make him go boom.

Arthur threw a pillow at the window, at the face of the distorted child. He threw the phone book, a coaster, several sachets of coffee and a blister pack of painkillers, before munching on a sausage. Fear left him ravenous, and there was the business of having locked himself in the larder for days.

"Surrender," the distorted face said, taking on the police officer's words. "Put down your bomb."

Behind Arthur, an insistent hand rapped at the door, offering no voice to identify the visitor. Arthur didn't open it. The face at the window pressed against the glass as if trying to melt through to the room. Arthur slid from the bed, on the door side, and clasped Lullaby to his chest. Both man and bomb sweltered, only Arthur offered actual sweat. Lullaby now fully understood he wasn't a child at all and was rather disappointed. He added volume to his tick to voice his dissatisfaction.

"I've come to collect your plates, sir," Lurch said, from the other side of the door. "And I'm to give you a letter from an angry man who is waving a gun at the hotel. I can tell you, the manager is not pleased and may ask you to vacate early."

As Arthur gibbered against the bed, still clutching Lullaby, a spider dropped from the ceiling and advised, "I'd open the door. Lurch doesn't like to be ignored."

Then the spider scurried towards the window, possibly to advise the distorted child to go away before they all blew to smithereens. The curtains fanned out, as if someone stepped behind them.

"Come on now, sir," Lurch said, knuckles continuing to rap against the door.

There seemed more of a scrape to Lurch's words now, as if he hoped to tear through the door with his teeth. Did he have a key? Arthur jammed Lullaby against the door. He needed to close the curtains. Draw them tight and climb into the wardrobe with the remains of his sausage and mash supper. The gravy was already beginning to congeal.

Despite Lullaby's best efforts, the door began to open. On the other side of the room, the face at the window pushed through glass and merged fully formed as three separate children. Arthur turned on the spot, bloodied shirt tails flapping. There was no escape. Above him, the ceiling fan began to whirr. Outside, a siren blared and people began to disperse.

"Shoo," Arthur said to the children. To Lurch he said, "Please stay out."

All ignored his requests. Backed into a corner of the room with Lurch advancing from the left and the children from the right, with Lullaby rolling into the hall and to freedom, sweat dripped from Arthur's nose, beaded on his eyebrows. All it took was the drop of an interested spider from the ceiling fan to end it all. As William 'The Terror' Craven balled a fist and aimed it at Arthur's nose, the spider's thread broke and it landed on Arthur's right eyeball. With the blink of a desperate eyelid, Arthur Charles Manfred Edwards exploded taking out his bald patch, the wardrobe, three phantom children and Lurch's hand.

In the hallway outside the smouldering room, Lullaby rolled towards the lift doors. They opened just as he reached them. A pretty woman in a red-spotted dress picked him up and cuddled him to her chest muttering something about hating porters, which was odd as Lullaby thought he'd like to be a porter when he grew up.

Cate Gardner

Wrath of the Deep

I

It wasn't much of a hotel room. Might have been once, but now the paint was faded, the plaster flaking, the paper peeling. A cracked window overlooked an empty promenade and a rocky beach where the grey sea heaved up and down like a grimy half-set jelly, foaming in the shingle. Another room in a run-down hotel at the edge of the city.

Kellett sat on the bed, craving a cigarette and staring at the mobile phone on the bedside table. When it finally rang, he made himself wait till the third ring: he wouldn't let Montague hear how desperate he was. "Hello?"

"Gregory," said Montague. "Enjoying your *vacances sur la plage?*"

"Having a whale of a time, Cuthbert. When are you getting me out of here?"

"Your loyal service hasn't been forgotten. You *know* I have a long memory."

Did he have to make everything sound like a veiled threat? But Kellett had no choice other than to play the game.

"It's hardly in my interest to let your ex-colleagues in the police catch you," Montague said. "Even with the best defence money could buy, they'll still throw the book at

135 "

you unless you offer them a bigger fish. And let's be honest, that means me."

"I wouldn't talk. I'm not stupid." However short the sentence, Kellett wouldn't live to see the end of it, not even segregated from the general prison population on Rule 45. Enough of the men he'd killed for Montague had friends and family who'd make sure of that. If Montague himself didn't.

"That's why you're still alive, Gregory. But have no fear. I'll ensure your safety, personally."

"Okay. What's the plan?"

"As you may or may not recall, I own a lovely little cabin cruiser called the *Odyssey*, and tomorrow night, I'll be taking her out – nothing like a little sea air, what? By coincidence, I'll be passing your particular stretch of coastline at around nine p.m. or so. If a chap happened to be on the beach around that time, he'd find a small dinghy coming ashore – are we clear?"

"Oh yes," said Kellett.

"The dinghy will bring you back, and after that, it's next stop Amsterdam. And you'll be disembarking complete with a nice attaché case containing a new passport and enough cash, in various currencies, to tide you over for quite some time to come. My advice would be to invest part of it in a business of some sort. Sound like a suitable golden handshake, dear boy?"

"Yes," said Kellett. "Perfect. Thank you."

"Good," said Montague. "Then it's a deal."

But still Kellett waited, knowing they weren't done yet. Montague was like a cat toying with a mouse – whenever you thought that the final *coup de grace* must come, he'd invent one last torture for his prey. "Subject, that is, to one condition."

Here it came. "What?"

"Call it one last favour. Nothing too onerous. Just someone I want you to kill."

II

"His name's Fraser," Montague said. "Professor Duncan Fraser. You won't find him difficult to find – or to deal with."

"For crying out loud, Cuthbert – I've got the cops after me as it is. And it's not as if my warrant card's going to help me out this time, is it?"

"You won't need it. You won't even have to risk your personal safety by venturing outside. I've made it all very easy for you, Gregory. You see, Professor Fraser, like you, is a guest at the Hyde Hotel. In fact, he's the *only* other guest currently staying at the Hyde Hotel."

"What? But that's–"

"After tomorrow night, you won't be here. You'll have vanished. I'm assuming you weren't so foolish as to book in there under your own name."

"Of course not."

"Well, there you are. Plenty of opportunity to observe your mark and time the hit to perfection. As for your getaway – well, just look out of your window."

Was this some kind of set-up? Kellett shrugged; it wouldn't be hard to make the hit look like an accident. "Anything else?"

"Yes," said Montague. "He's got something that I want."

"Okay. What am I looking for?"

"Ever heard of the lost city of Dunwich?"

"No. Should I have?"

"Unlikely. It was a major port on the Suffolk coast, until the thirteenth century. Storms destroyed the harbour and silted the estuary it stood on, and it spent the next few hundred years falling into the sea a little at a time. Anyway, it had a lot of churches. And one of those churches contained a little item – a sort of medallion or amulet. Solid gold, on a golden chain. It was kept in that particular church, under very close guard. High security, you might say, at least for the time. High enough that it should still have been there, under the rubble, all these centuries later."

"And Professor Fraser?"

"Professor Fraser has been fascinated, to the point of obsession, with Dunwich his whole life. He's mounted a number of diving expeditions to investigate what ruins still remain on the seabed, but he was struggling to raise the required finance this time out. So, I agreed to fund him – on one condition."

"That he got you this amulet." It didn't surprise Kellett. Montague had funny tastes, after all. Most impoverished aristocrats found other ways to deal with their cash-flow problems than human trafficking and the drug trade.

"Quite. And I know for a fact that he did. Unfortunately, he seems to have decided against keeping his part of the bargain. He's been on the run, and gone into hiding. But then I traced him here. And lo and behold, your little – ahem – problem arose and you needed a place to hide..."

"So you decided to kill two birds with one stone?"

"Exactly. Professor Fraser is in remarkably good shape for his age – he wouldn't be able to go diving otherwise – but he's still in his sixties. I'd hardly expect him to be a problem for you. I'm sure you can make it look like an unfortunate accident or *felo de se* easily enough – in fact, I'd rather you did. Just make sure you get the amulet and bring it to the beach tomorrow night. If you don't—"

"I get it."

"Good. Good. Until tomorrow night, then."

"Yeah," said Kellett, but he was already talking to a dead line.

III

He wandered downstairs, spent time in the TV lounge and the bar. He went outside, and smoked several cigarettes, one after the other, before going back in. He watched the sun sink and the sea darken, but there was still no sign of the professor. He kept an eye on the reception desk, but the hotel register was out of sight and it wasn't the kind of hotel that kept racks of room keys hanging up in plain view.

Short of quizzing the hotel staff directly, there was no way of determining where the professor was, and Kellett preferred to keep a low profile. It was bad enough being one of only two guests; he didn't like being anywhere near this visible. It solved the mystery of why Montague had told him to book in here, though. Kellett hadn't fancied it at all; there were all sorts of unsavoury rumours about the Hyde Hotel, although they were vague and contradictory, few of them even agreeing to its location.

Of course, with a place this dodgy the staff had hopefully learned the virtues of selective amnesia, but Kellett wasn't taking any chances he could avoid.

He went back upstairs; by now it was late and it didn't seem likely Professor Fraser would be coming down. Not to worry; he already had a game plan for tomorrow.

As a boy, Kellett had liked fishing, and he'd been good at it. It wasn't a game for the impatient; you had to know your enemy, prepare, and wait. It was about knowing the right bait and where to cast. Here for bream or tench; there for rudd and roach, chub and dace, here for barbel, there for perch. He knew the small fish too: bleak and ruffe, minnow and gudgeon. He'd loved the names as much as anything else; odd and alien in sound, no clue as to what tongue they'd been shaped from to name those sinuous, darting shapes in the water.

If you had a game licence there were others still – trout, salmon, grayling, eel – but for the coarse fisherman the ultimate opponent was the pike. Sleek, dagger-shaped and lethal, the tyrant of the waters, the pike found somewhere suitably concealing – a patch of dense waterweed, perhaps – and waited, still and silent, for its prey to come closer. And then, when it did, the fish bent its body into a Z-shape and struck, seizing hold with inward-pointing fangs that, once locked in place, never let go. They couldn't, even if the fish wanted to. If the prey was too big to swallow at a gulp, the pike swam around, digesting it bit by bit.

Hide, prepare, wait – and then strike once, and make sure the job was done. That was the pike's way, and it was Kellett's too.

In his room, he made coffee, then sat on his bed in the dark, listening. A creak sounded above him. Then another, and another. It was coming from the next floor up, he reckoned. Not quite directly overhead. A little to his left.

Kellett kept listening; soon another sound registered. A low murmuring. Then a second voice – thick, wet, snarling. Was the professor with someone? A member of staff, perhaps?

Kellett inched to his door; gently, gently, he eased it ajar. The low murmuring carried on. He strained and made out words: *patri, fili, spiritu sancti...* Maybe the professor was a Catholic.

The thick voice came back. Kellett found he couldn't make out a word it said, and he was actually glad he couldn't. Something about that voice made him want to hide from it, and so he did, shutting the door again, locking it and switching on the lights.

His room had a narrow, precarious-looking balcony, and the windows weren't supposed to open, but he forced them, flinching as he did – what if they set off an alarm? Luckily, they didn't.

He slipped a small leather wallet out of his suitcase. It fastened with a zip. The kind of thing you used to keep a netbook or a tablet in.

He went out on the balcony and sat on its damp grimy floor, his back against the flimsy balustrade, then pushed the window shut and lit a cigarette. He smoked it steadily down, then unzipped the wallet.

Inside was a thick sheet of foam rubber; set into the holes cut in it was a pistol, a silencer, a spare magazine and a box of ammunition. The gun was a .380 Beretta; it had a cutaway slide that ensured the bullet wouldn't jam, it used subsonic ammunition that worked well with a silencer, was compact, accurate and took a thirteen-round magazine. He prided himself on doing the job with a single shot whenever possible, but if anything went wrong he preferred having plenty of firepower to hand. The bullets had been dum-dummed, crosses cut at the tips so that they would mushroom on impact for maximum damage.

Kellett lit another cigarette and sat there for some time, the silenced pistol across his lap, alone in the dark.

~

The next morning, he was awake by seven a.m. Breakfast was served from eight through to nine thirty. He went down at five to eight and dawdled over his food till, at eight thirty, his prey arrived.

Kellett sipped his coffee and barely spared the professor a glance, but his heart-rate picked up sharply and he had to work hard to maintain the façade of being just another diner – a salesman, maybe, from out of town – munching his way steadily through his English breakfast, leafing through the morning *Telegraph* while watching Fraser via his peripheral vision.

Sitting in corduroy trousers, a food-stained check shirt and a shapeless old cardigan, Fraser looked sick and frail – tired, too, as if he hadn't slept all night. His eyes were bloodshot and dark-ringed, his grey hair disarrayed and he had two or three days of uncut stubble.

Alzheimer's, maybe, kicking in suddenly and out of

nowhere. Maybe the old boy had gone gaga and wandered off, still clutching this antique knick-knack Montague wanted so badly. But he'd remembered enough to check into a hotel. Did that make sense?

Maybe, maybe not. It hardly mattered. If he'd pissed Montague off, it wasn't surprising he hadn't had any sleep. The important part was his room number. Each table had a plaque giving the number of the room it served: Fraser's read 213.

Kellett finished his meal and went back upstairs to his room. He took out the Beretta, loaded it and waited for the tramp of ascending footsteps. When they came, he let them pass and fade, then slipped out of his room and tiptoed up the stairs. It didn't take him long to find 213. He leant close, and soon heard the murmur he'd heard last night, although he could still only make out odd words of Latin.

A moment later, he recoiled as the thick, wet voice spoke again. It too was pitched low, but its tone came through loud and clear: hateful, sneering, full of gloating venom.

Footsteps sounded further along the corridor: a maid probably, coming to clean the rooms. Kellett tiptoed back downstairs.

What *was* that voice? Was Fraser hiding a companion in his room? If not, perhaps he had a radio; it might be a broadcast he listened to, or perhaps he was in communication with someone else. Another buyer, perhaps, for Montague's precious amulet. If so, the old bugger was about to learn an important lesson in honouring business agreements. Not that he'd have the chance to profit from it.

More likely the poor old sod was completely doolally and talking to himself. Same result either way, and it probably qualified as a mercy killing. Certainly would compared to what Montague would have inflicted on Fraser.

Kellett pulled on his long coat, dropped the pistol into one of its pockets, and went outside. He pottered up and down the promenade, even along the beach, feet crunching in the shingle, but never out of sight of the hotel. Eventually he wandered back; in his room he disassembled and reassembled the Beretta, cleaned and oiled it, and waited. Once or twice he put his head outside the door; he didn't need to go any further to hear Fraser's rambling chant going on.

Evening came, and it was time. Kellett changed into a dark t-shirt and a pair of jog-pants he'd had time to pack before going on the run; good clothes for work that might get messy. Of course, he was fairly confident of this one being easy – but he hadn't lasted as long as he had by taking foolish chances.

Kellett tucked the Beretta into his waistband, let the t-shirt fall over it, and went up the stairs.

IV

The murmuring was still coming from Fraser's room when he reached the door. A quick glance up and down the corridor confirmed no-one was in sight; the only sound was from the professor.

No time like the present, then. Kellett pulled on a thin pair of nitrile gloves, slipped the Beretta from his waistband and held it flat against his thigh, then rapped on the door with his free hand.

The murmuring stopped. A silence, but no movement. Kellett rapped again.

"Who is it?" called a querulous voice. "What do you want?"

"Professor Fraser?"

"Who is this?"

"This is Mr Walton, Professor," Kellett said. "I'm the assistant manager. I just wondered if I might have a word."

"Well, this is not a good time."

"I'm afraid I must insist, Professor. We've had complaints from other guests about the noise from your room. If we can talk now, we can work something out – moving you to a different room, perhaps. But if not, I'll have no choice but to ask you to leave the hotel." A silence. "Professor?"

"Wait a moment."

Footsteps approached the door. The lock turned. The door opened a crack, revealing a half-shaved face and a bloodshot eye: it was Fraser, all right.

He might have recognised Kellett from breakfast; it didn't matter. Before he could react Kellett had a foot in the door, then had the silenced pistol aimed through the gap at the bloodshot eye. "Step back, Professor," he said, "keep your hands where I can see them, and don't make any noise."

Lips compressed, Fraser retreated into the room. Kellett slipped in after him, then heeled the door shut.

"You know why I'm here," he said.

Fraser's mouth twisted. "Montague."

"You promised him something and then you welched

on it." Kellett shook his head; he almost pitied the old fool. "What did you *think* was going to happen?"

"Your Mr Montague might thank me yet for trying to keep it from him," said Fraser. "And so might you."

Kellett shook his head. "I'm just a tradesman, passing through. And if you thought Montague was gonna be philosophical about this, you really should have got to know him better. He's used to getting what he wants."

"I can see that now."

"Bit late, though."

"Hm." The professor actually chuckled. "I don't think I need to ask what happens next, do I?"

Kellett shook his head. He was starting to warm to the old beggar; shame, really.

"Can I at least hope it will be quick and painless?"

"As long as you co-operate," said Kellett.

"Yes, that would seem reasonable enough. You want the amulet, I assume."

Kellett nodded again.

"My bedside table. Top drawer."

Waving him back, Kellett sat on the edge of the bed and reached for the drawer.

"There's a legend connected with the amulet," said Fraser. "Did Montague tell you?"

Inside was a lumpy object swaddled in oily cloth. "No."

"Very obscure tale. Supposedly a fisherman found the amulet in his nets, and took it back to Dunwich. But it belonged to the King Beneath The Sea."

"Who?" Kellett picked the object up. It was about the size of his fist; it was heavy, and clinked.

"That's all the story says. Of course, most pre-Christian faiths had a sea-god – the Greeks had Poseidon, the Romans Neptune, the Norse had Aegir and the Celts had Llyr…"

"I get the point."

"The King was angry; he followed the fisherman back to Dunwich. In those days it was the biggest shipping port in East Anglia, a major city. The King Beneath The Sea demanded the amulet's return, or he would destroy all Dunwich."

"Then throwing the thing back would have been the sensible thing to do," said Kellett, putting the bundle down beside him.

"You'd think."

"But let me guess – they didn't." Kellett began unwrapping the bundle.

"These old legends can seem quite queer to us at times," the professor admitted. "The characters' motivations are quite hard to understand. Maybe it was considered to be a case of finders keepers, or possession being nine points of the law. In any case, you're quite right. They said no."

Kellett saw a glint of gold. "So what happened?"

"The King Beneath The Sea summoned up a great storm, huge waves and assorted monsters of the deep to destroy the city. However, the local bishop was on hand; he called on God's help, and with it he drove the King and his storm back out to sea. And then he sealed the amulet in a reliquary in one of the city's great churches, as a proof of God's triumph."

There was a thick gold chain, wrapped around the

amulet. Kellett unwound it. "And they all lived happily ever after."

The professor smiled. "Not quite."

"Go on." Kellett turned from the amulet and gave the old man his full attention. The story had sort of caught his interest, and Fraser obviously enjoyed telling the tale. Might as well let him go out doing something he liked.

"The King laid a curse on Dunwich," the professor explained, "and soon after that came the great storm that destroyed the harbour. It was the end of Dunwich as a port, and the city began to fall into decay. In revenge, the bishop laid a charm upon the reliquary, so that the King Beneath The Sea would never find his amulet while it was sealed there. Over the years, the storms kept coming and the King's curse wore away the coast, until piece by piece, street by street and church by church the city fell into the sea."

"Hm." Kellett went back to unwinding the last of the chain. "So each side managed to fuck the other over. The King destroyed the city, but he never got his toy back."

"Pretty much."

Kellett held the amulet up on its chain. It was in the shape of a head, something with bulbous eyes and a vast mouth full of long, serrated teeth. It vaguely reminded him of some predatory deep-sea fish he'd once seen a picture of – hopefully the kind that had been extinct for several million years. Kellett wasn't much of a swimmer, but all being well he'd be some way out to sea in a few hours' time, and he could do without the thought of a monstrosity like this anywhere near him. "He's an ugly bastard, isn't he?"

Fraser didn't answer; that, and a flicker of movement in Kellett's ever-reliable peripheral vision, caught his attention just in time. The old man's hand had lunged into his cardigan pocket, thrusting something in it towards Kellett.

Kellett rocked sideways on the bed and fired twice. He didn't aim; at that range, he didn't really need to. The Beretta made two dull thuds, so close together they were virtually a single sound, and Fraser cannoned back into the bathroom doorframe, face twisted, before collapsing. His hand slid out of his cardigan pocket clutching a small revolver.

Kellett plucked the gun from the professor's fingers and tossed it on the bed. "That was very silly," he told Fraser. The bullet wounds, both in the man's chest, seemed bloodless at first, but as he watched, red stains spread out around them. He dragged the professor into the bathroom, bundled him into the bath, then went back to retrieve the empty bullet cases and wrap the amulet in its cloth before shoving it in his pocket.

When he went back into the bathroom, Fraser was still alive, though only just. His shirt and cardigan were a sodden red and so were most of his trousers; the floor of the bath was awash with blood, and pinkish foam was bubbling from the old man's nose and mouth. Lung wound, Kellett thought.

"You silly sod," he said. "Told you, co-operate and it'll be quick and painless. But you had to be clever. Now look at you."

Fraser stared up at him with agonised, dimming, pleading eyes.

Kellett sighed. "Okay, Prof. Can't blame you for trying, can I? And the story was all right." He aimed and fired a third shot, this time to the head, catching the ejected casing in mid-fall. Fraser's body jerked once, then was still.

Kellett shut the bathroom door, listened at the room door till he was sure no-one was there, then let himself out. The corridor was empty; a faded red carpet with a pattern that seemed to swim in the glow from the lights in Art Deco sconces, two lines of white room doors like gravestones. Nothing else. He slipped off the gloves, went down the stairs, and let himself back into his room.

Well, that was that. Not the neatest job he'd ever done, and not exactly what Montague had expressed a preference for. It certainly wouldn't look like an accident, and even if he'd left the Beretta at the scene, no-one was going to believe Fraser had killed himself. Kellett sighed. All his own fault; he'd let the old man's demeanour distract him. And he *had* ended up rather liking the man. A pity your targets couldn't always be bastards who deserved it. But the job was done, and in an hour or two he'd be away.

He changed out of the murder clothes and back into jeans and sweater, hid the gun away but kept it close, just in case. Then he unwrapped the amulet and studied it again. Ugly bloody thing. He tossed it down on the bed and started packing his clothes.

And then stopped.

Was there a television on somewhere? There must be; someone was laughing close by, and there was something *familiar* about it. Except that there weren't any other guests. Or could it be one of the staff? Kellett grew even stiller: could somebody have seen? He picked up the Beretta, went to the door, opened it...

...and looked out into an empty corridor.

He shut the door, locked it.

And the laughter grew louder. Then it stopped, and a voice spoke instead.

"Oh, you've gone and done it now," it said. It was deep and thick; it gloated and it sneered. That was where he knew it from; it had been coming out from under the door of Fraser's room.

But where was it coming from now? He couldn't have brought it with him; he'd only brought one thing down from there.

A low chuckling sounded. At last he pinpointed the source of the sound. It couldn't be coming from there. But it was.

Kellett sidled over to the bed, looked down.

And the gold face of the amulet leered and writhed; the gold eyes swivelled to focus on him. The mouth moved, and a voice came out.

"You've *really* gone and done it," it said.

V

"What *are* you?" Kellett said. He had a good two-handed grip on the Beretta and aimed it down at the amulet, realising as he did that he felt both frightened and ridiculous, all at once.

"What do you *think* I am, you blithering idiot?" Thick and wet though the voice was, it was also plummy and rich, like a well-marinated middle-aged actor. "You heard the story from Fraser – before you killed him, that is."

"You mean that was true? That legend? I mean, literally..."

The amulet rolled its eyes and snorted. "No. This is all a dream. Of course it was literally true."

Kellett didn't answer. Everything he'd ever known and seen and believed said that stories about a King Beneath The Sea, curses and pieces of jewellery that talked to you were idle amusements at best and outright madness at worse, and an hour ago he'd have agreed. But now he was being told otherwise, and by a fairly unimpeachable source. It's hard to deny the impossible when it's talking to you.

"What's your name?" said the amulet.

"Kellett."

"Well, Kellett, I'll explain things to you as I explained them–or tried to – to the late Professor Fraser. You can do yourself a great deal of good here. All you have to do is return me to the sea. It's very simple. You'll spare yourself a lot of hardship that way – and perhaps even earn a small reward into the bargain."

"Trouble is, there's a gentleman who's expecting to take delivery of you tonight," said Kellett. "And I'm relying on him for safe passage abroad and a plentiful dollop of change."

"So I understand," said the amulet, "but that isn't *my* problem."

"What kind of reward are we talking, then?"

"Oh... something along the lines of... your life, I would expect."

"You're really not selling this, are you?"

"Money and safe passage are valueless if you aren't alive to take advantage of them, Kellett. You'll grant me that, at least."

Kellett shrugged. The amulet had a point.

"As long as you keep me from my rightful owner, you put yourself in grave danger. You don't even have to throw me back into the sea yourself. Just... leave me. Tell Montague I was lost. That Fraser... discarded me, because he believed in the mad old legend of the King Beneath The Sea. Threw me back. It's close enough to the truth that he'd believe it."

"Why didn't he?" Apart from the not inconsiderable issue of Montague's displeasure, throwing the amulet into the sea was looking more attractive by the minute.

"Montague, pure and simple," the amulet said. "Fraser feared him almost as much as me. Perhaps even more, because he had a means of controlling me."

"He did, did he?"

The amulet laughed. "Don't get your hopes up, Kellett. How do you think the Christ-folk trapped me so that my master couldn't find me? Why, they closed me in a casket of silver, inside another of cold iron, then put that in a reliquary of stone. But most of all that vile Bishop laid a charm, a ward, on me – I couldn't call out, and neither my master nor his servants could locate me. A mighty incantation, it was, but it shut me tightly up – until the caskets were opened. Soon after that, I could have called to the King Beneath The Sea and he'd have come for me – and we'd have been reunited, at long, long last." Its voice had grown melancholy. "But Professor

Fraser, he knew that incantation too, and used it against me."

Patri, fili, spiritu sancti... "That was the muttering I heard?"

"Exactly. All from memory, as well. You won't find it written down anywhere in Fraser's room, if that's what you were thinking. He had to keep re-performing it, because without the silver and iron caskets it just isn't the same. And a professor of archaeology, however distinguished, is no substitute for a prince of the Holy Church." The amulet sniggered. "Which basically means that now there's nothing to stop me letting the King know exactly where I am. And trust me, Kellett, you don't want to be here when he, or whoever he sends, arrives."

"If I don't get Montague what he wants," said Kellett, "then I won't be any better off. How about a deal?" If anyone had told him he'd end up negotiating terms with a talking medallion, least of all in a situation involving Montague... "Let me hand you over to Montague. He's transporting me by boat. Once I'm off, call your boss and he can do whatever he likes. I don't owe Montague anything, the twisted fucker."

The amulet sighed. "Nice try, Kellett."

"What do you mean, nice try? It's a good deal."

"If Montague knows the legend – and I'd be astonished if he didn't – there's a good chance he'll know how to contain me."

"Come off it – you think Montague believes in shit like this? Any more than *I* did twenty minutes ago?"

"If you were me, Kellett, if you were enjoying one brief

window of freedom after centuries of confinement, would you take the chance of waiting till you were in the hands of your next owner and hoping he wouldn't know how to silence you?"

Kellett was silent again; put that way, the amulet left him with no answer.

"And before you suggest a reward, a finder's fee – I'm the King's rightful property. To him, paying to get me back would be acknowledging that you have a claim on me to begin with. Sorry, Kellett, there's a principle at stake here."

Again, Kellett had nothing to say.

"I'll give you one more chance," the amulet said. "Give me up, and you'll live."

He *could* tell Montague that Fraser had lost the plot and thrown the amulet away. It wasn't as if the police would find it in the dead man's room, or as if he'd have it on him when he boarded the *Odyssey*. But Montague had a way of sniffing out lies; more to the point, he had a way of dealing with failure, and the sea would make a very convenient burial ground. No; the best bet was to give him the amulet and hope for the best – hope that he and Kellett had parted company by the time the amulet's owner came looking.

"I'm sorry," said Kellett.

"So am I," the amulet said, with what sounded like genuine regret. Then the small eyes closed, the fanged mouth stretched wide and a low, deep sound came out.

Kellett raised the Beretta and fired. The bullet hit the amulet's open mouth and made it jump. It made a noise and he shot it twice more, both rounds thudding into the heavy gold. It landed back on the bed and lay there face-down.

Kellett breathed out. He picked up the empty cases. At this rate, he'd have a whole sackful of spent brass to dispose of. Better check how bad the damage was, he thought, and leaned over the bed.

Something flew up and hit him in the face; something small and hard. He reached for it as it fell to the coverlet, but as he did two more objects bounced off him and fell beside the first. He stared at them, then scooped them all up in his hand. Distorted and flattened by the impact but still recognisable, the bullets were still warm.

"That," said the amulet, "wasn't very nice." It lay face-up on the coverlet, showing no signs of damage. It spat again, as if to rid itself of the bullets' taste. Then its mouth stretched open once more.

Kellett didn't shoot again; instead he reached for a pillow as a low bass rumble began to sound – smother it somehow, silence it – but first the vibration was in his gut, his balls, and then it spread, till his whole body felt like a tuning fork. He was shaking so hard he thought he would come apart. He fell and grovelled on the carpet, tasting blood in his mouth, sure his head was about to explode.

Finally the sound faded. Kellett got up, shaking, and wiped his mouth and nose. He found blood on his fingers.

Kellett glared down at the amulet, and its fanged mouth warped into a smile. If it could have shrugged, he suspected it would have.

"He's sending someone," was all it said.

VI

Kellett checked his watch; there was half an hour to go before he met Montague's dinghy.

He reloaded the Beretta's magazine; God knew if it would do him any good or not, but he liked to be fully prepared.

He eyed the amulet, but it said no more, not even when he rewrapped it in its rags and stuffed it in his jeans pocket.

Other than that, his wallet and the gun, there was nothing he couldn't leave behind if he had to be fast. He'd have preferred to burn the clothes and gloves he'd worn when he killed Fraser, but if he had to leave them it wouldn't really matter, not if the coppers tracked him here. His prints were all over the hotel room and they'd know by now that a Beretta .380 was his weapon of choice, but Fraser's was just one more murder when they already had more than enough evidence to put him away for life. What mattered was staying ahead of them.

He was ready.

He peered out to sea from his window. A light gleamed a few miles out. A boat. Maybe it was Montague's, maybe not. He checked his watch again. Ten minutes to nine.

It was time.

He actually had his hand on the door when the amulet spoke again; its voice didn't sound at all muffled. "Where do you think you're going, Kellett?"

"I've got a boat to catch."

"Do you really think so, Kellett?"

The first thing he registered when he opened the door

was the smell. It was a cold, briny stink of seaweed, dead fish, and stagnant air.

The second thing was the cold; the next breath he drew in seemed to scorch his lungs and when he breathed out, it hung pale in the air like smoke.

The third thing was the figure down the corridor.

It stood between him and the top of the stairs. He knew, of course, that it was the source of both the stench and the cold. It was very tall, well over seven feet in height, and *dark*. He couldn't make out any features in detail, only its silhouette – except for its eyes, which were round and luminously gold.

It seemed to be wearing a long coat or cape that reached down to the floor, and its head must be abnormally high, given how close to its shoulders the eyes were. It rose high and separated into two crowns; vaguely man-shaped though it was, it wasn't human, couldn't be.

The amulet was laughing. "Do you think you can get past him, Kellett? And he's just the first of many."

The figure stood silent and still. Kellett aimed at it two-handed. "Okay, pal, step aside."

It just watched him.

"I don't want to kill you," Kellett said.

"That's a laugh," said the amulet.

"Shut up–but I will if I have to."

"I think you mean you'll *try*."

"Shut up!"

The amulet laughed.

Kellett stepped forward, and the thing from the sea glided forward to meet him. "Stay where you are," he said, but it came on.

Kellett fired. Two clean shots, aimed at the centre of its mass. If you couldn't get a headshot it was the best place to aim; you'd a good chance of hitting the heart, and even if the target moved the chances were you'd hit something important. But the thing barely twitched, and Kellett might have imagined even that.

He fired two more rounds into its body, then aimed between the golden eyes and fired again – then higher, into the twin-domed head. The shape jerked a little, but still came on, and now there was a sound – a low, rattling hiss – and its eyes' glow brightened.

"Fuck you too," spat Kellett, and fired out the pistol before ducking back into his room and slamming the door. He dumped the spent magazine, pulled the spare out of his pocket and slammed it into place, aiming at the door, waiting for it to fly open.

It didn't; what happened instead was somehow worse. There was a hissing sound, then a sizzling, and a smell of burning wafted into the room. The paint on the door began to blister and char, and a shape formed; that of the thing from the sea, burning through the doorway.

The hotel's fire alarm shrilled; it snapped Kellett out of the paralysis the sight had held him in. He snatched up the chair that stood beside the bed and flung it at the window, full force. The glass exploded. Kellett knocked the jagged splinters from the window frame with the Beretta's silencer, then climbed out onto the balcony, thrusting the gun through his belt.

He looked back once, in time to see his bedroom door burst into flame. Then he was climbing over the parapet and hanging by his hands from the bottom of the balcony, legs swinging to and fro before he let himself drop.

He hit the balcony below his room with a thud, rolling, slamming against the window. Good thing there was nobody there. He looked down. A two-storey drop he wouldn't have chanced, but one? Not a problem.

Lights were blinking on in windows down the seafront. Kellett climbed up on the parapet and jumped, hit the pavement, rolled and came up running. He felt more athletic than he had in years; danger did that to you, and he'd done his best to avoid tasting it for a long time. Still, you could never eliminate it entirely from the life he led, so it provided a welcome rush, like speed.

He ran across the promenade, vaulted on top of the sea wall and leapt. He crashed and rolled over the shingle, floundering to his feet; it was harder to be fast on this loose slope. He chanced a look back at the Hyde Hotel; smoke was billowing from the balcony of his room, and a tall black shape loomed out onto it.

Kellett ran down the beach to the thin white line of breaking surf. A torch flashed out to sea, played across the waves towards him. He ran into the water, gasping at the searing icy bite of it – *the King's domain*, he thought, *all this belongs to the King, talk about out of the frying pan and into the fire –* as it rose to shins, knees, thighs and groin. Fuck, that hurt.

But there was the boat – a rubber dinghy with an outboard motor, just as Montague had said, with a lean, tough-looking man minding the tiller. Kellett recognised him from the little the moonlight showed of his face: an ex-Army type called Newell.

Kellett scrambled aboard. Newell cursed as the

dinghy lurched and rocked, almost tipping over. "The fuck do you think you're playing at, you–"

"Never mind that," Kellett gasped, "just get us out of here."

Newell was staring past him towards the seafront. "What the hell happened there?"

"Just *go*," shouted Kellett, following the man's gaze in spite of himself to the hotel and the figure on the balcony. The golden eyes were tiny glittering embers from here, but they found him in the dark, and he knew that they saw. "Go," he said again.

Even as he did, the shape on the balcony sprang forward. It leapt over the parapet, hung suspended for a moment, then fell.

Briefly.

Its cloak or cape spread out – wide, like wings. It fell, then rose, bouncing on the wind, and then it swooped, sweeping down over the road, the promenade and the beach, towards them.

"Fuck me," said Newell.

"*Go!*" screamed Kellett, and at last the other man responded; the dinghy's engine roared into life, it swung round in the water and rushed out into the gathering dark of the sea.

VII

Up ahead were the lights of the *Odyssey*; Newell aimed the dinghy at them and gave the engine full power. He didn't resist when Kellett took his torch, shining the powerful beam back over the water at the diminishing lights on the shoreline.

"What the fuck was that?" he demanded at last.

"Something that wants a certain item almost as much as Montague does," said Kellett. He drew the Beretta and checked the action. "You armed?"

Newell nodded, lugging a heavy pistol from a shoulder holster. The two of them peered into the dark between them and the shore, but saw nothing but the dimly lit water. Kellett unscrewed the silencer from the Beretta and after a moment, tossed it overboard; it would just get in the way now. "It's got to have a weak spot somewhere."

"Better find it fast, then," said Newell. "Thing was going like the clappers."

Montague's boat was in sight now, a sleek white shape aglow with lights. A tall figure came out onto the deck. Nearly there. If they were lucky, Montague might know something that could help them. If not, they might at least outpace the opposition long enough for Kellett to go his way, after which the amulet would be someone else's problem.

Newell glanced back, saw they were nearing their destination, and cut the engine's power so the dinghy slowed to a halt beside the *Odyssey*.

Montague leant over the rail; fair-haired, blue-eyed, the face of a handsome schoolboy, with a shotgun propped on his shoulder. "Ah, Kellett. I assume you have something for me."

"Yup." Kellett patted his jeans pocket; he thought he heard something snigger. He pushed the Beretta into his belt.

"Good," said Montague. "Welcome aboard."

A rope ladder was tossed over the ship's side; Newell reached for it.

And the thing from the sea flew into the circle of light from the *Odyssey* and snatched him off the ladder.

Newell screamed; in the same moment there was a muffled bang and the dinghy lurched, pitched and crumpled. Kellett had enough time to see that something had ripped the vessel almost in two before he was in the water and floundering to keep afloat, reaching desperately for the ladder's bottom rungs.

Above, Newell screamed again. Kellett looked up. There was a sound like wet cardboard being torn and the screaming stopped. Newell fell out of the sky – in two pieces, one falling on either side of the boat.

"Christ!" said Montague.

The amulet bayed with laughter. "Should have listened to me, shouldn't you?" it called. Kellett grabbed the ladder rungs and climbed.

The thing from the sea wheeled, and for a moment he saw it clearly against the moon. The closest he could come to a description would be to call it some nightmare hybrid of bat and octopus, each tentacle tipped by a curved, serrated talon and with a dark membrane stretched between them.

Its gold eyes found him, and it dived. Kellett clawed for the Beretta, but knew there was no chance.

A hollow boom sounded, and the thing flew sideways in the air, screeching and flailing. It thrashed and gained height again; nearly half its tentacles hung limp and useless, the membrane between them shredded.

Montague walked to the *Odyssey*'s stern rail and

pumped the slide of his shotgun. The thing flew at him; he pumped two shots into it, then leapt aside as it struck the rear of the boat. It collapsed across the railing like a deflated balloon, then slid off into the water. As Kellett climbed aboard, Montague aimed down and fired two more rounds into it; Kellett reached the stern rail just in time to see the thing's ragged, tattered remnants slip beneath the surface.

"Well," said Montague, thumbing fresh cartridges into his weapon, "that was… interesting."

"What the hell did you have in those shells?" said Kellett. "I put a full clip in that thing and it barely noticed."

"Steel shot, old boy," said Montague, and walked to the bridge. The *Odyssey's* engines revved into life, and she pushed out into the open sea.

"Of course," breathed a barely-audible voice from Kellett's jeans. "Iron is always an effective bane. Apparently steel works just as well."

Kellett said nothing. He fumbled his cigarettes from their packet. To his surprise, most of them were still dry.

"You know that's only the first, Kellett," the amulet said. "The first of many."

Kellett turned away, leant on the railings, lit a cigarette as the black night-sea swept past, hands shaking as they hadn't done in many years and kills.

He blew out the last of the smoke, flicked the cigarette butt into the water and walked to the bridge, where Montague stood with his hands on the wheel. "Thanks," he said.

"Protecting my investment, old chap. Do you have something for me?"

"Yeah." Kellett fished out the amulet; he was tempted to throw it overboard, but didn't. He handed it to Montague and walked aft. The coast receded; the town's lights blurred, merged and were lost to sight.

He was still at the rail when the grey dawn showed, to reveal an even greyer and emptier sea. He reached for his cigarettes again, but before he could light one Montague said "Gregory?"

Kellett knew, even before he turned, from the tone of his voice, even before he saw the shotgun. He should have known from the start, really; perhaps, deep down, he had. This was cheaper by far than a new passport and a bagful of money, and far more certain to ensure a permanent silence. He'd only trusted Montague because he'd had no other option.

He knew all that; knew, too, as he reached for the Beretta, that he'd never be in time. The shotgun fired and Montague vanished in a bloom of smoke and flame: something smashed into Kellett and carried him back against the railings. The Beretta bounced under the rail and into the sea. *Goodbye, old friend*. Blood and severed fingers lay on the decking.

Montague walked to Kellett and tipped him over the side. Kellett fell headfirst into the water and bobbed back up again. He wasn't sinking yet, but neither could he move.

Montague smiled and gave him a mocking salute, then walked back to the wheelhouse. The *Odyssey* pulled away. Kellett managed to turn his head to watch it go.

Then the water he lay in dropped suddenly; up ahead of the boat it rose, in a great wall-like wave. As if something vast was either rising from the depths in front of the *Odyssey* or opening its jaws underneath.

The first of many, the amulet had said. From far, far away he heard its dark wet laughter, heard Montague curse and scream. Kellett started laughing to drown out it out, and was still laughing when his lungs filled up with blood.

Simon Bestwick

The Sealed Window

Hoffman hated the city and he was sure the feeling was reciprocated.

Each time he visited – sometimes for work but often at Monica's insistence, to visit the theatre or friends or simply shop – it was always hot and filthy and far too crowded. He hated the fact that everywhere he turned, he was pushed or pulled, cajoled or pressured, swept up in clouds of perfume or body odour and baked in the hothouse atmosphere the canyons of concrete created.

Now that Monica was gone, in a flurry of poorly chosen words, vicious recriminations and slammed doors, he hoped his visits would lessen exponentially.

But not today, as he was dragged back to the morass. As his train pulled into the station, he gathered his overnight bag from the storage shelf, feeling the sheen of sweat on his back and he wanted to laugh at the insanity of it but two hours in a quiet coach listening to the tinny bass-heavy music from three seats back wouldn't let him.

A meeting had been called for middle managers last week at work. You need to do some training for the J-Sox requirements, they said. There's a course running in the city, they said. You can stay overnight, they said. And he'd stood in the office, listening to his weasel-faced boss extol the virtues of going away for a night on the town at the company's expense and wanted to smash his head onto the blotter on his desk.

The company he worked for had been swallowed up, a couple of years before, by an American concern. Monica had been the one to make him see it as encouraging, that with the additional funding it would strengthen the company standing and she was right. But then the American parent company had been swallowed up by a Japanese behemoth just around the time things had started to go sour with Monica and now, in Hoffman's mind, it was all melded together into one awful mindfuck. Even worse, complying with Japanese accounting policies meant a whole lot of new knowledge was needed.

The train came to a halt and all of the passengers around Hoffman tried to get up at once. He turned, to see who it was with the headphones and noticed a young woman, her hair three shades of purple, pulling on a slim rucksack. Two earbuds on white leads ran out of the neckline of her vest.

Hoffman pushed his way into the aisle, aiming in the direction the headphone girl was going, but the gap between them quickly increased. And anyway, he thought, what would he have done if he'd caught her? Told her off for playing her music too loudly on a quiet coach? He was forty years old, so he already looked terribly dated to her and his saying something that stupid would surely unleash a torrent of abuse.

Leave it, he thought, just let it go. But if he did that, the situation wouldn't be rectified or revised and nothing would ever change until it wanted to. He was always leaving things, hoping for the best but knowing that they'd soon fall apart.

Hoffman got off the train and followed the herd through the ticket office to the main doors. As he stepped outside the heat of the day seemed to rush and embrace him, like a hot blanket that wanted to cover every inch of him. He felt sweat bead on his forehead and top lip. A young couple, all dreadlocks, vests, hiking boots and funky backpacks, pushed past him into the station, their skin glowing with sweat.

"Fucking brilliant," he said and walked over to the taxi rank.

~

"The Hyde Hotel?" asked the taxi driver, with that sounded like disbelief in his voice. He inclined his head against the rest but didn't turn to look at Hoffman.

"Yes," Hoffman said and double checked the paper Alice in the office had given him. "The Hyde Hotel, on Beaumont Street."

"Fair enough," said the driver. He flicked the meter on, put the seen-better-days cab into gear and pulled away. Hoffman managed to bite his lip for all of five hundred yards.

"Is there something wrong with The Hyde Hotel?"

"Not at all, mate."

"So why did you question it?"

"Did I?"

"Yes, before we pulled off."

"Can't remember, mate."

Hoffman sat back in his seat and shook his head,

catching the driver's eyes in the rear view mirror. The man had definitely said the name as a question, as if there was something wrong with it. Was it a flophouse? Had there been a mistake in the office and rather than being in a pleasant, executive hotel he was in some dive in the arse-end of nowhere? That would be his luck, certainly.

The traffic came to a halt. "Bit warm, ain't it?" asked the driver.

"Uh huh."

"Can't stand the heat meself, hate driving the cab in it. The wife loves it, first bit of sun we get, she's out in the garden and cooking away."

"I don't like it either. It always seems worse in the city."

"Oh aye," said the driver, "it's all the brick and glass, we're in an oven here."

"When you get home and shower, your hair is full of grit and carbon."

The driver grunted, as if he hadn't understood and Hoffman didn't want to explain. The traffic began to move and he leaned his elbow on the window-sill, resting his chin in his hands. The people outside moved with sluggish intent, as if the heat were seeping them of their will and drive. Skin glistened, clothes featured dark spots at arms and smalls of back.

The taxi took a sharp left and the driver pulled up at the kerb.

"Here you go," he said.

Hoffman paid, waited for a receipt and got out of the cab, the heat of the day embracing him once more. He was standing on the wide pavement of a narrow street that seemed to consist of boutique stores and blankly anonymous offices accommodated in turn of the century town houses. The Hyde Hotel, in front of him, was no different. There were six large windows, all of them apparently a storey high, running along the street and looking into the restaurant and reception. The glass looked clean until he got closer, when he could see the streaks and the small bits of grit and grime that had accumulated in the corners. The second floor windows were smaller and all of them had yellowing nets obscuring the view. The hotel seemed to have had an extra floor built into the mansard roof and the electric sign, saying 'Hyde Hotel' above the door crackled, as if it was on its last legs.

As the taxi drove away, Hoffman extended the handle of his overnight case and walked into the foyer. As the revolving doors shushed away the outside world, he was hit by the cool air and the calm. Nobody shouted, no cars could be heard, just the hum of polite conversation and air conditioning. A very tall man, wearing a claret-red uniform, stepped out of an alcove and nodded.

"Can I help you, sir?" the man asked, his voice slow and deep.

"No," said Hoffman, "I've just come to book in."

"You have a reservation?"

"I do, my office made it."

The man made an elegant bow, holding his left arm away from him. Hoffman followed the line and saw the reception desk across the deserted foyer. He made his way over, the lush carpet silencing his footsteps. Behind the desk was a large rack of numbered boxes, some with keys hanging on them but most of them empty. To either side of the rack was a door, the one on Hoffman's left said 'Private' and the other 'Manager'. Both were closed. Behind the desk, standing but looking down and hunched over slightly, was a balding man. He was wearing a pale blue shirt and a red tie.

Hoffman reached the desk and the man didn't look up. After waiting a few moments, Hoffman cleared his throat but the man didn't move. Hoffman pulled his case forward so that it clunked gently against the desk but still no reaction.

"Hello?"

It took a moment for the man behind the counter to look up. "Yes?" His pate was completely smooth, but the hair around the sides and back was thick and grey and full of some kind of oil. He had a long face, dull eyes that looked too small and a long nose. His mouth was a tiny slash, his lips the only real colour in his face.

"My name's Hoffman, I'm booked in for the night."

"Of course you are, sir," said the man without looking at anything to confirm it. He reached behind him and delicately picked a key from a box, arching his back slightly. When he turned, the strain to reach showed as red spots on his pale cheeks. "Room 339, up to the third floor. Do you want a hand with your bag?"

Hoffman frowned. The man had been looking down when he came in and the desk now hid him below the chest, so how did he know there was only one bag? "No, I'll be fine."

"Up the stairs then," said the man, pointing behind Hoffman, "away you go."

Dismissed, Hoffman accepted the key and turned back towards the main doors. Arching up above them on either side were two wide flights of steps. How had he not noticed them before when the doorman pointed to the desk? Had the heat got to him that much?

~

At the third floor landing, Hoffman pushed open the double doors. A corridor ran to either side of him, doors on both sides, evens facing the front, odds facing him. An ornate sign in front of him indicated that 30-35 was to his right, the remainder to his left.

He turned into the corridor and was taken aback that the end of it was almost impossible to see, a spot of a vanishing point. He turned, looking behind him and saw the same thing, the corridor stretching on for hundreds of yards. The ceilings were high, a good three feet above him and covered with ornate mouldings and the light fittings were clusters of delicate white glass shades spaced a few feet apart. The room doors looked heavy and sat snug in their wide frames.

"Not bad," he said quietly, "not bad at all."

A few feet ahead of him was an occasional table, with a highly polished silver pot on it. Inside were the remains of a spider plant, the fronds black and clearly dead and bugs walked in the pale earth. Hoffman shook his head and made his way to his room and, as he did, realised the perspective of the corridor was changing. The ceiling was getting lower, his headroom much reduced and he could see the vanishing point of the corridor was a painting on the wall.

By the time he reached number 339, the ceiling was less than a foot from his head. He unlocked the door – how quaint to have a key in this day and age – took one last look down the corridor and then stepped in.

The room was very small and very warm and he instantly didn't like it. To his left, against an otherwise blank wall, was a vanity table and a double-fronted slim wardrobe. A small flat screen TV was on the table, a rectangular mirror mounted on the wall above it. Straight ahead was another blank wall with one small window, set at chest height. On the right side was a doorway and a double bed, above it an abstract image that might have been a ball, a flower or the moon. A narrow bedside cabinet had a lamp and telephone on it.

"Oh fucking hell," he said and hefted his overnight bag onto the duvet. He walked around the end of the bed to the window and pulled back the net curtain. The window was perhaps four foot across and two down and his view consisted of the wall of the building across an alleyway. He couldn't even see the sky. Hoffman pushed his finger under the mechanism and tried to open the window, some fresh air would be better than none.

The window mechanism didn't move. He pushed and pulled at it but nothing happened. The more he pushed and pulled, the hotter he became and the hotter he became, the more conscious he was that he had no fresh air in the room. He could feel tendrils of claustrophobia flickering at the edge of his mind but tried to brush them aside.

Giving up, Hoffman laid on the bed and reached for

the phone. A sticker on it, written in calligraphy, advised he dial 0 for reception. He picked up the receiver and was surprised to see the phone had a rotary dialer.

"Yes?"

"Hello, this is Mr Hoffman in room 339."

"Yes?"

"I have a problem with the room, I can't get the window open."

"It sometimes sticks," said the man on reception, "I'll send someone up."

"Fine, thank you."

Hoffman sat on the edge of the bed. From here, he could reach to his left and touch the wardrobe and if he leaned forward, he could touch the bottom of the window.

"This room isn't big enough," he said, got up and went into the bathroom. It was half the size of the main room with a toilet, sink and bath that had a shower unit over it. There was a small narrow window high up on the back wall and it was open slightly. He stood underneath it and tried to push it open further but it had been painted to stay open.

"For fucks sake," he said and went back into the room. He looked at his watch, saw it was past five and decided to go and get something to eat. He wanted to spend as little time as possible in this room.

~

It was after nine by the time Hoffman got back. The foyer of the hotel was deserted – no doorman to greet him, no receptionist behind the desk – and he trudged up to the third floor feeling hot and annoyed. The streets had been heaving with people, all of them locked into their phone screens and not caring where they walked or who they walked into. The couple on the next table in the lovely little Italian restaurant he found spent their entire meal engrossed not in each other, but in their phones, pausing only to fork in fresh mouthfuls or photograph their food when the orders arrived.

He walked along the corridor, the carpet swallowing the sound of his progress. The fancy work on the ceiling looked different now but he couldn't tell why. He paused at door 339 and debated going back out, to avoid spending too much time in the hot little room but, then, maybe the window was fixed.

Hoffman quickly opened the door and went in. The first thing he noticed was a heavy bleach smell, the second was that the window hadn't been opened. He walked over and tried the handle but, if anything, it moved less now than it did before.

His anger simmering, he flopped onto the bed and reached for the phone. He dialled reception and the phone rang for two minutes and forty-two seconds but nobody answered it. The ambient heat in the room, combined with the heat his own anger was generating, made him feel even worse and with a growl he stalked into the bathroom.

There was no smell of bleach in there, which surprised him. The partly opened window let in a little fresh air and he glanced at the bath, which looked spotlessly clean. He went back into the room, got his toilet pack from the overnight bag and had a long, cool shower.

~

It was 10.15 when he came out of the bathroom, a towel wrapped around his waist. The temperature in the bathroom, heated up by his shower, was doubled in the main room and he could feel fresh sweat in his hairline and at the small of his back. He tried the window again but it wouldn't move. The smell of bleach had disappeared.

Hoffman took a deep breath, trying to calm himself. If he got wound up, if he allowed himself to get angry at the weather and the sealed window and the tiny room, he'd get hotter and nothing would get better. He dug through his overnight, found his paperback and lay naked on top of the bed. The faintest of draughts blew through the bathroom window and door to brush his skin gently.

He opened the book and started to read. It was an old thriller novel he'd found in a secondhand shop and normally the sleazy shenanigans were enough to keep his attention but he found he couldn't focus now. Three times he read a single line.

He heard a noise, like heavy machinery moving into gear. He sat on the edge of the bed, listening and realised it sounded like a lift coming to the floor. But he hadn't seen a lift.

There was a ping.

He stood up and walked to the door.

Voices sounded in the corridor, a man and woman. They were talking in drunken whispers about their night out. Hoffman groaned and got back on the bed, pulling open the paperback and trying to read. He listened as his neighbours

– amidst much shushing of each other – got the door open. The woman said something he couldn't make out, a long question that the man answered with a curt and loud "no."

"Terrific," said Hoffman.

In the time it took him to read a chapter, his neighbours had had a discussion, a shower and got into bed. He could hear the murmur of their conversation and wanted to hammer on the wall and yell 'shut the fuck up'. But he didn't, he draped the book on his chest and closed his eyes. The room was still very warm and each time he moved, his skin was stuck to the top sheet.

The woman next door moaned.

Hoffman debated going for another shower but knew the heat would just get worse.

The man next door said something and the woman moaned even louder.

Hoffman rolled onto his side. The man next door did something that the woman particularly liked, if her squeal of delight was anything to go by. Hoffman rolled onto his other side, trying to shut out the sounds. It was impossible, of course but he stared at the page until the words ran into one then looked up and out of the window at the darkness beyond.

The woman next door grunted and there was a clatter against the wall. Hoffman heard something click and the woman squealed, before the headboard hit the wall again. Another click.

"Now," he heard the man say.

"No," squealed the woman, "no, not that."

There was a loud crack, which sounded to Hoffman like a slap. All sound from the next room ceased, as if the noise had startled them too. A few moments later, he heard someone crying. The headboard rattled against the wall and the woman grunted again.

"Oh pissing hell," said Hoffman and he gave up on the book, hotching down the bed to switch on the TV. It took a few beats to warm up and he flicked through the channels – BBC One and Two, ITV and Channel 4, the BBC news channel. After four stations of static, he found a murky looking film, as if it was being broadcast from a dodgy VHS tape with the tracking askew. Five more stations and he could hear someone shouting in a foreign language but had no picture.

Another slapping sound from next door, followed by more silence.

Four more channels and he got another murky picture. It cleared into a pin-sharp image, then degraded again. It seemed to be a film, a man and a woman sitting in a diner. Judging by the fashions and hair, it seemed to be from the seventies but he couldn't be sure.

"Don't you fucking make fun of that!" yelled the man from next door.

"Fuck me," said the woman on the TV. She was now leaning over the table in the diner, her face inches away from the man. "Fuck me hard and never stop."

"I'll fucking do what I want!" yelled the woman from next door and the slapping sound came again, followed by a burst of the headboard rattling against the wall.

On the TV, the man and woman were now on the diner table, she almost naked, him down to his underpants. The camera moved to get a better angle and Hoffman could see his huge cock standing proud.

The woman next door grunted. "Fuck me like you mean it," she said.

The room felt hotter now, as if there was a radiator hidden somewhere turned up to full. Hoffman switched off the TV, annoyed that his own cock was responding to the visuals and crossed to the window. Gripping the handle firmly, he wrenched it backwards and forwards until he heard plastic crack but the thing didn't move at all. He pulled the net away so hard it came away from the window and, angry with it, threw it behind him. Beads of sweat ran down his temples and back and the backs of his knees were sticky. He wanted to scream, it was all getting too much and his ability to cope seemed to have abandoned him – whether it was Monica, next doors activities or being trapped in an airless room in the city he didn't want to be in.

The couple next door had now found their rhythm and the headboard was banging against the wall with metronomic monotony. Hoffman leant against the wall under the window and slid down, his face in his hands. He could feel the clamminess of his skin, could see the sheen of sweat on his belly and legs.

There was a loud thud from the wardrobe, startling him. He looked at the unit but the doors were still closed.

Next door reached a fresh plateau of ecstasy.

He stood up and walked over to the wardrobe. It was a plain thing, nondescript to the point that he knew he wouldn't be able to describe it by this time tomorrow. He put his hand on the veneer door, instantly leaving a sweaty print there and reached for the handle.

Hoffman pulled it open and saw the man instantly. He

was almost on his knees but the belt, looped around his neck and tied to the clothes rail, wasn't quite long enough. The leather of it had dug into his skin and his eyes were wide open and bulging. Blood coated his lips and ran in little channels down his chin and onto his bare chest.

Shocked, Hoffman staggered back until the bed hit the backs of his knees and he fell. The wardrobe door swung shut and the couple next door erupted into a fresh bout of grunting and slapping. It took a moment or two for his heartbeat to steady and as he sat up, the top sheet peeled away from his back.

Was it even possible that he'd really seen what he thought he had? As much as he knew it wasn't, he had to look in the wardrobe again, he had to be sure. Was that what had left the bleach smell, where someone had been trying to clean something up? He stood up and gingerly reached for the door handle. His clammy fingers closed over the warm metal. He pulled, gently.

The wardrobe door swung open and all he could see was a mirror fixed to the back of it, his own naked reflection staring at him. He looked at the floor, saw the scrub marks and could smell the bleach now.

Was that it? Had someone, the last guest perhaps, hung themselves in the wardrobe?

The couple next door began to bounce the headboard off the wall with such intensity it sounded like they were punching it. Hoffman closed his eyes, tried counting to ten but it didn't help. The day had been getting progressively worse and their noise, their inconsiderately loud fucking, was just enough to tip him over the edge.

He pulled open the door and stepped into the corridor, intending to burst into their room and tell them exactly what he thought. But he froze as soon as his feet touched the thick carpet. Everything was wrong, as if a child had been let loose at a draughtsman's table. The ceiling undulated back towards the staircase, a wave moving along its length as he watched. The mouldings ebbed and flowed, as if breathing, and he could hear the clanking and wheezing of a lift system that had no door, that wasn't even installed. To his right, the forced perspective painting was now circular, coils of lights disappearing into themselves and each other. His mind span, trying to grasp everything and he could feel a pain at the back of his head.

Hoffman put his hand against the wall and felt his fingers slide into the material, the plaster like sludge. He quickly pulled his hand back, checked it and shook away the doughy material that was dissolving into his skin.

Back into the room, he slammed the door and leaned against it. The heat was worse, if anything and he felt fresh sweat run out of his hairline. Pushing himself off the door, his skin peeling away with a horrible wet sound, he realised the couple next door were silent now. He felt a wave of nausea ripple through him and knew he was going to be sick. He staggered around the bed, his hands clasped over his mouth, aiming for the bathroom. He'd just reached that door when the room door was flung open, bouncing off the wall.

Hoffman turned and saw a stranger in the doorway. He was short and round, a well-padded stomach hanging over his genitals though Hoffman could see the man had a raging erection.

"You've put me off my stroke," snarled the man and he rushed around the bed.

Hoffman clattered into the bathroom door and fell, sliding along the Lino until he came to rest beside the bath. The plastic felt blissfully cool against his shoulders and neck. He rolled over, meaning to walk on his hands and knees to the toilet but the bathroom door burst open and the naked man stood over him.

"Didn't like our fucking, eh?" he screamed, his face red, spittle flying from his mouth. He leaned over, his arms by his sides and there was insanity in his eyes.

Hoffman couldn't push back any further and the nausea was welling inside him. "No," he said, instantly hating himself for being so weak and hating the man more for putting him in this position.

"No?" bellowed the man, his face getting redder. Spittle was collecting at the sides of his mouth now and his eyes were becoming bloodshot.

There was nowhere for Hoffman to go. He'd had enough, with the situation at home and being here in the city and being too hot, he wasn't going to take it any more. Bracing his shoulders against the bath, he drew up his legs and then kicked them out, digging his heels into the man's shins. The man screamed and fell to his knees, clawing at the air pointlessly. Hoffman pushed himself backwards, his sweaty back sliding up the plastic. The man grabbed for him again, fingers brushing but not quite catching Hoffman's face and shoulder. The man got to his feet, hobbling and took a step towards the bath.

Hoffman kicked out again, higher this time, feeling the man's testicles crush under his heel and the movement pushed him backwards, sliding him into the bath.

The man howled like a wounded dog and fell forward, his hands cupping his crotch. Too late, he saw the edge of the sink and by then there was nothing he could do about it. Hoffman watched as the man's teeth connected with the edge of the basin, his downward force snapping and cracking some of them as the man's weight pushed his face against the porcelain. As his body dropped, his head snapped back and something, like the sound of a twig snapping, happened in the man's neck.

The man hit the floor and didn't move.

Hoffman lay in the bottom of the bath, trying to catch his breath. It was cooler here than anywhere else in the room and he liked that, decided he'd stay for a while.

He knew that if he sat up the man wouldn't be there, knew it as much as he knew there was no bleach in the wardrobe, no woman handcuffed to the bed next door, no weird geometry going on in the corridor. He knew it as clearly as he understood that night followed day, and that it was the disgusting heat making him hallucinate.

He knew it as clearly as he understood that Monica hadn't just chosen to walk out on him, that she'd been guided by his apparently good friend Kevin. That when he'd called around to see Monica last night, in a final attempt to win her back, he'd seen Kevin's car in the driveway. The front door had been on the latch so he'd let himself in, listening to the sounds of their rutting which guided him upstairs and to their bedroom. To the bed that he once shared.

Hoffman had stood in the doorway for a while before Monica saw him and screamed. Kevin had leapt straight off, there'd been a fight on the landing and a lot of things had happened. A lot of blood had been spilled, more than Hoffman would have thought possible. It'd taken him an hour to tidy himself up.

He replayed those images in his mind until he was happy and then pushed himself up in the bath. Hoffman's first surprise was that the man was still on the floor, blood pooling around his head. His second was hearing the main door open and someone come in.

"Hello?" asked the woman, "is anyone there?"

Mark West

The Blue Room

The room was entirely blue. The walls were deep cerulean and the carpet was the colour of cornflowers. The bedspread was lavender, covered in a patchwork quilt of turquoise and teal, dotted with forget-me-nots and irises. The furniture had been painted in varying shades of blue; the dressing table a baby blue with amethyst drawer knobs, while the wardrobe was almost navy, heavily lacquered so that you could see your outline in its panels. Even the dainty cups and saucers, sporting a chinoiserie design gleamed a cobalt blue.

In fact Gwen was hard pressed to find anything in the room that wasn't blue. She rummaged along the sideboard, flicking through the hotel literature, the list of local attractions, all printed on powder blue paper with the Hyde Hotel crest embossed in Royal blue ink. She was surprised to find such attention to detail in such a modestly priced hotel. She had expected magnolia walls, tired flat pack furniture and laminate fire safety notices pinned on the walls. But this felt more like some chic boutique hotel. She sat down on the bed, laughing at her good fortune. It was about time the universe relented a little.

Instinctively, she opened the bedside drawer, expecting the customary plastic bound New Testament, but even the bible had not escaped the blue treatment, encased in a bright periwinkle jacket. It seemed appropriate, not only because it conformed to the décor of the room, but because she knew that blue was the most sacrosanct of colours. The tour guide at the Scrovegni Chapel had said as much, when she and David had honeymooned in Italy all those years ago. She could still bring to mind Madonnas cloaked in blue, gazing out from canvases and frescoes. It was hard to imagine that this colour, extracted from lapis lazuli, had been such a revelation when it was first introduced to the Italian masters. They had never seen such a blue of such vibrancy before. But lapis lazuli was extremely expensive, so rare that the Church claimed exclusive rights to it, even banning ordinary people from wearing the colour for a time.

Gwen sat down on the bed. It was hard to imagine a colour being outlawed. But then she thought about how much colour she used to wear before she was married. She'd even gone through a phase of having bright streaks of blue or pink in her hair. David was the eccentric. He preferred her to dress a little more conservatively and before she knew it her rainbow wardrobe was replaced with polyester skirts and white blouses. She rubbed the white material of her shirt between her fingers and with a sudden urgency began to undo the buttons.

She made her way to the bathroom, intent on continuing her inspection. A cursory glance confirmed her expectations: blue tiles, blue towels and a blue bathroom suite. Anywhere else, a blue bathroom suite would have been terribly outmoded. But somehow here, already immersed in so much blue, it seemed strangely elegant, stylish even. She cast her blouse on the floor and closing the bathroom door behind her, saw the crow for the first time.

It was actually a woman and a crow but the crow was so black against the blueness of the painting, in the blueness of the room, that it stood out. Though it was only a print, Gwen could see the heavy black brushstrokes, the suggestion of feathers, talons spread wide. But the crow appeared docile, immobile, allowing the woman to caress it, resting her long fingers against its black wing, administering a kiss, as you would on the forehead of a child.

It was a curious composition. And a curious place to hang a print, behind a door, where no one would see it unless the bathroom door was closed. And how unusual for the door to open outwards in the first place. The bathroom was rather cramped; a lot of old hotels in order to accommodate the modern demand for en suites had to be inventive with their use of space. It couldn't possibly be arranged so just to conceal a painting. Gwen leaned in close and saw 'Picasso 1904' in the bottom right corner. It was not at all in the abstract style she associated with Picasso, or with his typical vibrant colour palette. It was so melancholically blue.

Suddenly exhausted, Gwen made her way to bed, but not before leaving the bathroom door wide open. She didn't want to look at this strange painting tonight; she didn't want to think about the crow bringing the blackness in, threatening to taint such an immaculately blue room.

~

Gwen woke to the scent of lavender, a memory of summer days and clear blue skies. She stretched remembering where she was. In the blue room. A room that even smelt of blue. She nestled deeper into the covers, feeling herself enveloped in blue seas, in gentle Mediterranean sunshine. Looking up, she saw how bright the ceiling was in the daylight. A Giotto ceiling like the one in the Scrovegni Chapel. The colour of heaven, except that this one wasn't dusted with gold stars.

She sat up and realised that she'd slept in her clothes. Her case was still by the door, and she was suddenly annoyed at herself for not unpacking the night before. All her clothes would be creased, not that she could remember what she'd brought anyway; she'd packed in such a hurry.

There was a typical lack of colour when she opened the case, so she opted for the least creased of her blouses and skirts and got dressed. It didn't seem to matter in the blue room, they gave a blue warmth to the muted, bland tones but stepping out into the hotel lobby she was suddenly aware of how washed out she looked. Invisible almost. But beyond the blue room, she saw that the rest of the hotel was fairly ordinary too. She had arrived the previous night in the dark and had barely taken in her surroundings. Now she saw that the décor was distinctly average: Artex magnolia walls, tired dado rails, worn carpets. The dining room was as uninspiring, except there'd been an attempt to brighten each of the tables with a vase of plastic red carnations.

Gwen sat down at a table next to the window, not that she could see much through the greying nets. At least the service was prompt, which was surprising considering how old the server was. He handed her a laminate menu.

"Good morning," Gwen said, the cheerfulness of the blue room was still with her despite her disappointment with the rest of the hotel. "I think I'll have the full English," she said after glancing through the options. "I'm famished."

The waiter stared. Gwen wondered if she should repeat her order. He was surely too old to be working still. She shifted under his gaze and looked about the room. She saw that the other patrons were staring too. Gwen smiled nervously.

"Tea or coffee?" the waiter said recovering.

"Coffee, please," Gwen replied and the awkwardness lifted as the waiter took the menu back. The other guests seemed to be going about their business as if nothing had happened. Perhaps she'd imagined it. Perhaps it was normal being a little paranoid. It was the first time she'd been out without David in many years. The first time she'd ever stayed someplace on her own. She loosened the collar of her blouse, feeling suddenly hot. The aroma of fried food, the insipid magnolia room filled with even blander diners made her queasy. She longed for the calming influence of the blue room. Just thinking of its turquoise walls, its lavender sheets relaxed her; so that by the time her coffee arrived she was perfectly in charge of her nerves.

It was then that she realised, looking around the room at the diners tucking into their breakfasts, why they had all stared. The Hyde Hotel clearly attracted a certain type of person. Mostly on their own, its patrons were nondescript, plain types, dressed in unassuming clothes. Lacking colour. But Gwen wasn't one of them anymore. The blue room had leant her some of its colour and she couldn't help but stand out.

~

The sky was the colour of oyster. It reminded her of the woman in the Picasso painting, with her sallow grey colouring. Strangely, as she walked through the busy streets, she couldn't help but seek out the blue tones of the city, in shop fronts, billboards, passing cars. Even the pavement beneath her feet possessed a bluish tincture in the drizzle. There was so much blue in the world, she'd never noticed it before. It was as if her eyes were suddenly open to a hidden palette, attuned to the blue in everything, and she felt its presence awakening something inside of her.

She made her way into a park, eager for a reprieve from the hustle and bustle and the feeling of sensory overload. She made her way along the tree-lined paths, past dog walkers and joggers, kids on bikes and scooters. She tried to see past the blue, to take in other colours but they were pale in comparison. She sat down on a bench and closed her eyes, but a blue mist swirled in her mind like a tempest.

When she opened her eyes again she noticed the woman on the bench opposite. She was hardly noteworthy, except for a blatant absence of blue; in fact a lack of any colour at all. Gwen stared more intently. Though the woman was dressed in beige and brown, she didn't seem to emit any colour at all. Not like the people she'd seen bustling through the city or the city itself, which radiated its presence in loud, blue tones. This woman was invisible.

In confirmation, a group of youths passed her by without notice, flanked by a couple of dog walkers who similarly ignored her. Even the dogs, yapping at the feet of passers-by, skirted past the woman as if there were nobody there. Perhaps there wasn't, at least nobody of any consequence. But Gwen could see her. She could see the way her shoulders hunched, the way she sat crumbled into the bench, a sense of sadness in her anonymity. How many invisible women were there in the world, sitting on park benches just like this one, their colour drained out of them by others, siphoned off so that they had none left for themselves? Slowly disappearing into a world that was too bright for them.

Gwen thought to go over. She had some blue now; perhaps she could lend her some of it. But as she made to move, a crow landed by the woman's feet, cawing loudly, undaunted by her presence. As if it were a rallying call, another flew down and another, until the woman was surrounded by a sombre black assembly. What were a flock of crows called? Was it a murder? How morbidly appropriate, Gwen thought as she watched them encircle their victim.

~

Back in the blue room, Gwen ran a bath. She wanted to be immersed in blue. As she sank into the water, she embraced the feeling of abandonment, of surrendering to the room, to its calming, sympathetic power. She hadn't expected to see Picasso's woman, but with the bathroom door open she could make out the painting's reflection in the veneer of the wardrobe. She thought about getting out of the bath and closing the bathroom door, but she could only see part of the painting and thankfully not the crow. It was just the woman. Seen through the navy panelling her appearance was almost ghostly, the tilt of her head seemed to imply supplication and her long hand was positioned as if in prayer.

Gwen felt tired. She sank deeper in the water, wondering idly how many people had drowned in their bathtubs, lulled into a watery sleep. She wondered if this had ever happened here at the Hyde, whether in all its history, some poor cleaning woman had discovered a pruned, blue corpse doing her morning rounds.

Gwen pushed the idea from her mind as she forced herself under. It is hard not to float she realised. It's an act of will to make yourself a dead weight. Lying against the bottom of the tub, Gwen opened her eyes and watched the bubbles stream up to the surface. It felt so good, this entirely blue world. She didn't see why she should come up at all.

A sudden screech pierced the water. Gwen bolted upright, already doubting whether she had heard anything at all. It had sounded like a shriek, an abrupt, short vocalisation, but the water was good at distorting things. Perhaps it had been a noise in a neighbouring room, or out on the corridor. The water had a way of cushioning sound, it could likely have been a bird at the window, cawing like the crows she'd seen in the park.

A blue woman walked past the doorway.

Gwen instinctively jerked backwards, water sluicing over the edge of the bathtub. She may have doubted the sound but there was no disputing this. A naked woman had just walked past the bathroom door. And this woman was now in her blue room.

Gwen froze as the realisation sank in. Should she call for help, alert the hotel staff somehow. But she was naked and vulnerable and she'd have to go through the blue room to get to the exit. Besides, Gwen had seen the grey blue hue of the woman's flesh, an intensity of tone that couldn't be down to the blue of the room alone.

Gwen didn't move. She listened hard but no sound came from the blue room, no footsteps, no opening of drawers or cupboards. It was as if no one was there.

Gwen stayed in the bath until the water was cold. Then she was finally roused by familiar sounds, of a television blaring from a neighbouring room, a trolley squeaking along the corridor outside. When she stepped out into the blue room she knew there would be nobody there. She'd already accepted that she had hallucinated the woman, that she had conjured her out of the blue mist in her mind.

Gwen sat down, wet and cold at the baby blue dressing table. She could barely see herself in the mirror through the condensation, so she wiped the glass gently with her fingertips, watching as cold droplets ran down the surface. She noticed the blue anaemic hue of her hands from so long in the water. Her lips too were a shade she recognised as the same unearthly pallor of the blue woman.

~

Gwen sat in the hotel restaurant, nursing a cup of coffee. The waiter hadn't stared so much this time, though she still noticed glances from other guests. At least she wasn't invisible any longer. She thought of the woman on the park bench, how even the crows had regarded her as an irrelevancy. Crows were scavengers weren't they? It was no coincidence that they conjured morbid associations; they sensed the nearness of death.

"Are you enjoying your stay?' the waiter asked, placing down the slice of cake she'd ordered. Despite his age, he still managed to sneak up on her.

"Very much so," Gwen replied, sitting taller, pleased to be engaged in conversation. "I have the most wonderful blue room. I wonder why the hotel doesn't boast about it more, it's a real selling point."

'Blue?'

"Yes," she said finishing her coffee. "Entirely blue".

The old man looked confused. He probably didn't get to the rooms very often, Gwen thought. He was probably confined to the restaurant and kitchen. Either that or he was likely going senile.

"My husband was a painter," Gwen found herself confessing. "He was always obsessed with colour."

"Hell," the old man said, as he reached for her cup with an unsteady hand.

"Pardon?"

"Blue is the colour of Hell, in some ancient mythology, I forget which one."

Gwen watched him knit his brows as he tried to

remember. Shrugging, he turned away, the tray cluttering as he made his way back towards the kitchen.

~

Gwen couldn't sleep that night. She couldn't stop thinking about the blue woman. The daylight had helped her to rationalise what she'd seen – the steam had perhaps given the impression of things that were not there, things that her exhausted mind had clung to – but now it was night, it was harder to convince herself that the blue woman had been the product of an overactive imagination. She'd felt so real.

Gwen could almost see her now. Walking across the blue room, stepping into her dreams, naked and brash. How confident the blue woman had been, striding across the room. Not huddling along and creeping the way invisible women did.

It was very likely the Hyde Hotel was haunted. Of course it would be with so many people coming and going. Hotels often harbour intense emotions, emotions that can't always be played out at home. How many lovers had the hotel seen, those involved in illicit encounters, deceiving someone they loved back home? And how many lonely desperate people had arrived at its door? Home to them was nothing but a torment; the Hyde Hotel was a brief reprieve, a refuge while they figured out what to do next. The residue of all of this must have accumulated like dust along the banisters and behind the wardrobes. Perhaps sometimes in a certain light, in a blue light, you could see it swirling in the air like a mist.

Gwen stared at the ceiling. Like Giotto's, minus the stars. As close to heaven as that master could envisage. But all she could think of was the old man's words. Was this really just a well-decorated hell?

Hell or not, it was beautiful and Gwen found herself melting into the blue. As if she were back in the bath, she let herself sink down into it, she could feel it envelop her and hold her in its secure blue warmth. There was no need to keep her head up anymore.

She slept like a child. As one safely nestled beneath blankets, a lullaby sung close by. She half-woke with this feeling of security, of someone resting against her, holding her tight.

"David," she murmured, rolling into him. And in her half-sleep she had already forgiven him. It was so much harder being on your own. The warmth of another is sacred, like the colour blue. Though you're never aware that you agree to the terms of such an exchange, sometimes it is worth losing your colour for someone else. You don't mind as they shine brighter, siphoning off your colour, you don't even object because they are at your side. That's the vampiric nature of love.

"David," she said again, moving towards him, needing to kiss him.

But the lips she touched were cold.

Opening her eyes, Gwen saw in the midnight blue room, the deathly pallor of those lips, and she realised it wasn't David but the blue woman at her side.

She recoiled, half expecting the blue woman to vanish before her eyes, but instead she sat up in bed, bringing her knee up so Gwen could see her blue sex. Brash and bold, wanting to be seen. Gwen stumbled out of the bed, falling against the floor, and she ran from the blue room.

~

"I'd like another room please," Gwen asked. "I don't care what colour, red, green, pink. Anything but blue."

The concierge pursed his lips together. He glanced down at the register and shook his head. "I'm afraid we are fully booked."

"You don't understand, I can't go back in there."

The concierge was indifferent and Gwen was suddenly aware of her frantic, bedraggled appearance, the lateness of the hour. She folded her arms against her nightdress, smoothed down her hair.

It was then she realised there was a woman at her side, a woman that had a set of hotel keys already in her hand, a small suitcase at her feet. In her urgency, Gwen had jumped the queue. She felt a pang of guilt that she hadn't noticed the woman, that she hadn't even seen her. The woman hadn't objected and Gwen realised that she was probably used to being ignored.

Feeling admonished and foolish, Gwen stepped back from the desk, but not before the woman reached out for her.

"It was only a nightmare," she said in a small voice.

Gwen nodded, and slowly made her way back to the blue room.

~

It wasn't the blue of Giotto's ceiling that greeted her the next morning, but the blue black of Picasso's crow. Gwen could see the painting from where she lay and it was almost as if the tones of the canvas had seeped out into the room. Everything appeared to have taken on a black tinge, becoming a few shades darker. She got out of bed and began to dress.

She supposed she should have been thankful that David had taught her a rudimentary appreciation of art, that she could comprehend this space that she now found herself in. It was hard not to absorb his passion. But she wondered about the passions of her own that she'd forfeited. Had she had some, before she'd gotten married? Or had she always been a blank slate? She rubbed her head, feeling a blue haze gathering there.

She made her way down to breakfast. It is easy to spot the invisible women when you were one yourself. The woman she'd seen by the concierge's desk the previous night was sat huddled in a corner, dressed blandly with her shoulders sagging. Trying to draw as little attention to herself as possible. Like the woman on the park bench, there was no colour about her at all. She was barely there.

Gwen made her way over. She had thought that she was gaining a little of her colour back, if only the colour the blue room had lent her for a time. But the reappearance of the blue woman had her doubting her perception. It had felt so easy when she'd first arrived in the blue room, immersed within its secure blue walls but now the blue was changing, getting darker and letting things in she didn't want to see.

She sat down opposite the woman, who recoiled slightly at seeing her.

"Do you mind if I join you?" Gwen asked, though she'd already made herself comfortable.

The young woman nodded, sipping her tea timidly.

"So what colour is yours?" Gwen asked.

"Excuse me?"

"Your Hell?"

"Sorry?"

"Your room, what colour's your room?"

"I'm not rightly sure," the woman replied. "Green, I think. I've only just arrived. I haven't taken much notice."

It was understandable; she'd arrived in the dead of night with only a tiny suitcase. She didn't look like a businesswoman and she had that nervous, hunched look Gwen was familiar with. What was she running away from?

"They have a lovely blue room," Gwen began, "the curtains are the colour of bluebells and the bedspread is cornflower with forget-me-nots on the coverlet. The lampshades are midnight blue and the ceiling is one of Giotto's own," she added, leaning in close, "minus the stars."

"Hmm," the woman smiled.

"But you can imagine those." Gwen felt the need to reach out to this woman, the way the woman had reached out to her the previous night. She took her hand and saw that she had a little colour after all. A band of bruised yellow imprints dotted her wrist. The woman snatched her hand away.

Gwen stood. "You can have the blue room when I'm gone."

~

Gwen ran a bath. She was sick of the blue room and its capacity for trickery, but it was the only place for her to go. Besides, she felt so exhausted with it all, she just wanted to sink into the water and stay there forever. Maybe, when she eventually resurfaced she'd be back in Italy with David, standing beneath the vault of the Scrovegni Chapel, gazing up at the stars. But she knew that couldn't happen, so she might as well just stay beneath the water, immersed in her cold, blue world.

She forced her body under and watched as the bubbles raced to the surface. There was a multitude at first, but then they become more sporadic, until there was no air left in her lungs. She closed her eyes against the blue and welcomed the black instead.

A screech jolted her awake and opening her eyes she saw a black smudge dart across the surface of the water. She bolted upright, breathing hard, gulping in air while wiping the water from her eyes. In the blue haze, she'd thought she'd seen a bird fly out into the blue room. It would be a crow, she knew, sensing the nearness of death. Then she heard laughter, soft giggling and moaning. She stepped out of the water carefully, leaving a trail of wet footprints on the blue tiles, and following the sound made her way into the blue room.

There were at least a dozen blue women, rolling around naked on the bed and floor. Each in variety of erotic embraces, kissing and caressing one another and flaunting their blue nakedness for all to see. Was this the Hyde's past? Was this a ghostly echo of the lovers who had been here once, strangely resurrected for Gwen to see?

It was then that she noticed the suggestion of the man at the epicentre. In the middle of this swirling blue orgy, she could see him plain as day, painted black like the crow in the painting. Heavy brushstrokes obscuring his heart, the one he had pledged to her.

Gwen recoiled from the scene, from those young, willing, blue bodies. She had ignored them before, but here they were, all together, swirling around and around like the lovers in Blake's 'Circle of the Lustful', condemned to some endless, purgatorial re-enactment. It wasn't the ghosts of the Hyde's past but the women – the models – that David had invited into their marriage, into their bed.

The room began to spin, with David at the centre of this crazed colour wheel. But the room wasn't blue any more; it was black. Gwen stumbled backwards, as the women seemed to take flight, encircling her like a murder of crows. They were crows, the lot of them, black-souled for what they had done to her. The blackness seemed almost absolute now and she knew with a feeling of clarity, that when she fell the crows would pick her corpse clean.

~

Gwen woke to a loud knocking.

"Room service," she heard and picking herself up from the floor, she managed to call, "Can you come back later?"

"I need to make up the room," the voice insisted.

Gwen made her way over to the door. Her body ached, not just from sleeping on the floor; it was as if she were only suddenly conscious of the tender feeling of her muscles and flesh.

"There's no need," she called through the door, "I'm going to check out." Though only just deciding, her body seemed to relax a little at the idea. She heard the cleaning trolley squeak past.

It was undoubtedly time for her to go, time to leave the blue room behind, but as she turned she saw that the room wasn't blue any longer.

It was magnolia, comprised of tired flat-pack furniture, worn carpet, dowdy soft furnishings and laminate fire safety notices.

Gwen rummaged along the sideboard, through the cupboards and drawers. Where were the chinoiserie cups, the amethyst drawer knobs, where was Giotto's vault? But only a pitiable Artex ceiling gazed back.

Had she made it up, like Yves Klein when he made his famous blue? But at least his blue had been real. Her blue was nothing but a haze, a strange vapour that despite its subtleties and nuances had evaporated into thin air. The room was entirely different; nothing of her blue period remained, nothing except the Picasso painting.

It was just as it was, the woman leaning over the crow, planting a solemn kiss on its brow. But it didn't seem quite so morbid now. Gwen had interpreted it to be about the strange allurement of death, but now she saw there was gratitude in the kiss, it was the kind of kiss you would give before bidding someone farewell.

Gwen sighed, taking in the new room and sat down slowly at the dressing table, a dressing table that wasn't baby blue at all, but fake wood veneer. The sight in the mirror was even more startling, and though she wanted to withdraw from what she saw there, she knew she had to confront it, now that the blue haze had lifted.

In the stark light, she saw the black blue of herself, the marks he had left on her that made others stare. She wasn't thankful for these colours, though they made her see herself more clearly. And knowing then that she would eventually get her colour back, she watched as the crow that had been on her shoulder the whole time, flew away.

V H Leslie

Checking Out

You wake from a troubled sleep, during which the night-time sounds of the Hyde seemed to leak not just into your room but into your dreams. You are glad you can't remember too much of them.

The bed sheets are damp with your sweat; you have thrashed around so much in the night it looks like someone else has slept alongside you. Your head aches despite not drinking, you don't fancy breakfast despite not eating the previous night. As you get up you have the faint but insistent feeling that something is different about the room compared to last night, but you can't pinpoint what. It is still the generic budget hotel you envisaged, there are still no mirrors, the window still won't open, and there is still nothing but decaf next to the kettle.

You hurriedly shower then dress, and leave the room with a nagging feeling that you have left something behind in there despite the fact that you never even properly unpacked. You undergo the same baffling journey through the Hyde corridors before you can find the reception desk to check out, as if the layout of the place had changed overnight.

"Hope you enjoyed your stay," the receptionist says. "I hope the Hyde lived up to your imaginations." He must mean 'expectations' – a lot of hotel workers are not English nowadays, after all.

When you step outside you feel an obscure feeling of release, of escape even, but you are too tied to examine its cause. Your phone finally finds a signal and a chirping sound alerts you to the fact that your appointment, your whole reason for your stay in this city and in the Hyde, has been cancelled.

Your walk from the hotel to the train station takes you as long as the day before, and none of it seems familiar. But you seem to have thrown off your fever and your appetite is coming back.

When you are finally in a part of the city you recognise, and the sun is higher in the sky than surely it should be, someone stops you in the street, a young man with an English accent.

"The Hyde Hotel?" you say. "Yes, it's back that way and left onto Low Pavement and…" You have no idea if the directions you are giving to this man are right, or right for him, and he looks dubious as if he has already been looking for it for some time.

"Thanks," the man, who is carrying the same holdall as you, says. He sets off in a different direction to that which you told him. "I imagine it's down this way."

James Everington

About the Guests

Simon Bestwick once roamed the Lancashire wilderness, wild and free, until a cunning lass from Liverpool charmed and trapped him before carting him off to Merseyside. He is now adapting to his new environment while writing feverishly. He's already responsible for the novels *Tide Of Souls* and *The Faceless*, and the story collections *A Hazy Shade Of Winter*, *Pictures Of The Dark*, *The Condemned* and *Let's Drink To The Dead*. In addition, his serial novel *Black Mountain*, which was published in ebook form by Spectral Press in 2014, will appear as a single volume in 2016, where it will join two new novels, *Hell's Ditch* and *Redman's Hill*, in a bid for world domination.

Ray Cluley's work has been published in *Black Static*, *Interzone* and *Crimewave* from TTA Press, *Shadows & Tall Trees* from Undertow Press, and *Icarus* from Lethe Press, as well as featuring in a variety of anthologies. Some of these stories have been reprinted for Ellen Datlow's *Best Horror of the Year* (volumes 3 and 6) and Steve Berman's *Wilde Stories 2013: The Year's Best Gay Speculative Fiction*. A couple have also been translated into French and Polish. One of them even won a British Fantasy Award. His most recent work includes *Water For Drowning* from This Is Horror and *Within the Wind, Beneath the Snow* from Spectral Press. His collection, *Probably Monsters*, was released in 2015 by ChiZine Press. You can find out more at probablymonsters.wordpress.com.

Alex Davis is an author and anthology editor based in Derby. His first novel, *The Last War*, was released in July 2015 from Tickety Boo Press and begins a trilogy of titles exploring the origins and earliest days of an alien race, the Noukari. He also had a range of short stories published in 2015, as well as a host of anthologies forthcoming as editor. You can find out more at **alexblogsabout.com** and on Twitter **@AlexDavis1981**.

Cate Gardner was born in, raised in, still lives in, and wonders if she will ever escape Liverpool. Her fiction has appeared in numerous places including *Black Static*, *Shimmer* and *Postscripts*. She has also had five novellas published; her fifth, *The Bureau of Them*, appeared in 2015 from Spectral Press.

V H Leslie's stories have appeared in *Black Static*, *Interzone*, *Weird Fiction Review*, *Strange Tales IV*, *Best British Horror* and *Best British Fantasy*. She has also had fiction and non-fiction published in *Shadows and Tall Trees* and is a columnist for This Is Horror. She was recently awarded a Hawthornden Fellowship and the Lightship First Chapter Prize. Her debut short story collection *Skein and Bone* (Undertow Books) was released in 2015, and 2016 will see the release of her novella *Bodies of Water* as part of the Remains series from Salt Publishing. More information on the author can be found at **vhleslie.wordpress.com**.

Alison Littlewood is the author of *A Cold Season*, published by Jo Fletcher Books, an imprint of Quercus. The novel was selected for the Richard and Judy Book Club, where it was described as "perfect reading for a dark winter's night." Her second novel, *Path of Needles*, is a dark blend of fairy tales and crime fiction, and her third, *The Unquiet House*, is a ghost story set in the Yorkshire countryside. Her fourth and fifth novels, *Zombie Apocalypse: Acapulcalypse Now* and *A Cold Silence* were released in 2015. Alison's short stories have been picked for *The Best Horror of the Year* and *The Mammoth Book of Best New Horror* anthologies, as well as *The Best British Fantasy 2013* and *The Mammoth Book of Best British Crime 10*. Other publication credits include the anthologies *Terror Tales of the Cotswolds*, *The Spectral Book of Horror Stories*, *Where Are We Going?* and *Never Again*. Alison lives in Yorkshire with her partner Fergus, in a house of creaking doors and crooked walls. Visit her at **alisonlittlewood.co.uk**.

Amelia Mangan is a writer originally from London, currently living in Sydney, Australia. She is the author of a novel, *Release* (Nightscape Press, 2015), and her stories have been featured in many anthologies, including *Drag Noir* (ed. K.T. Laity), *Attic Toys* (ed. Jeremy C. Shipp), and *The Grimorium Verum* (ed. Dean M. Drinkel). Her story, 'Blue Highway', won Yen Magazine's first annual short story competition in 2013 and was featured in its 65th issue. She can be found on Twitter **@AmeliaMangan** and Facebook at **facebook.com/amelia.mangan**.

S P Miskowski's four-book series, the *Skillute Cycle*, is published by Omnium Gatherum. Her stories have appeared in *Black Static*, *Supernatural Tales*, *Other Voices*, and *Identity Theory*, and will appear in the anthologies *October Dreams II*, *Cassilda's Song*, and *The Leaves of a Necronomicon*.

Iain Rowan lives in the north-east of England, near the sea but not near enough. He's had over thirty short stories published in magazines and anthologies, and his crime novel, *One of Us*, was shortlisted for the Crime Writers' Association Debut Dagger. He's just written his first screenplay, for a short film being made in summer 2015, and runs an active writers' group, Holmeside Writers.

Mark West was born in Northamptonshire in 1969 and now lives there with his wife Alison and their young son Matthew. Since discovering the small press in 1998 he has published over seventy short stories, two novels (*In The Rain With The Dead* and *Conjure*), a novelette (*The Mill*), a chapbook (*What Gets Left Behind*), a collection (*Strange Tales*) and two novellas (*Drive* and *The Last Film*). He has more short stories forthcoming and he is currently working on a novel. He can be contacted through his website at **markwest.org.uk** and is also on Twitter at **@MarkEWest**.

About the Proprietors

James Everington mainly writes dark, supernatural fiction, although he occasionally takes a break and writes dark, non-supernatural fiction. His second collection of such tales, *Falling Over*, is out now from Infinity Plus and a six part monthly serial, *The Quarantined City*, from Spectral Press. He has had work published or forthcoming in *The Outsiders* (Crystal Lake), *Supernatural Tales*, *Morpheus Tales* and *Little Visible Delight* (Omnium Gatherum), amongst others. He has a black cat and cream carpets, which shows how much thought he puts into those parts of his life that aren't book-related. Oh and he drinks Guinness, if anyone's asking. You can find out what James is currently up to at **jameseverington.blogspot.co.uk**.

Dan Howarth is a Mancunian born writer, now living on Merseyside and experiencing horror first hand. Dan's fiction has previously been published online and he has a story in *No Monsters Allowed* (edited by Alex Davis). He is deputy editor at **thisishorror.co.uk**, where he also helps run their print line.

www.ingramcontent.com/pod-product-compliance
Lightning Source LLC
Chambersburg PA
CBHW031014190726
48286CB00003BA/835